CATHOUSE CHAOS!

In the parlor the whores were screaming, running for the stairs, calling for Mrs. Kessler. Morgan jumped over the counter and saw Nelly running down the hall. He grabbed her by the hand and pulled her after him. A gun fired behind them and a bullet ripped into the front door and he turned and saw Mrs. Kessler steadying a double-barreled derringer for a better shot. . . .

Also in the *Buckskin* Series:

BUCKSKIN #14

LEVER ACTION

KIT DALTON

LEISURE BOOKS NEW YORK CITY

A LEISURE BOOK®

May 2004

Published by

Dorchester Publishing Co., Inc.
200 Madison Avenue
New York, NY 10016

ISBN 0-8439-2420-9

Visit us on the web at www.dorchesterpub.com.

BUCKSKIN #14

LEVER ACTION

ONE

Coming over the top of the pass, heading for home, Lee Morgan looked for the chimney smoke of Spade Bit in the distance. They had been away for a week, buying horses. There were heavily-timbered ridges between the pass and the ranch, but the sky was blue and cloudless and he should have been able to see smoke drifting up from the cookhouse and the main house. There was no smoke.

"What's up?" Sid Sefton asked, riding up to where Lee had reined in his horse. Bud Bent, Charlie Potts, and Wesley Ford were moving the newly bought horses down from the pass.

Lee pulled his hat brim low to shade his eyes. "I don't know," he said. "You see any chimney smoke down at the ranch? There should be some smoke."

Sefton squinted against the sun. "Ought to be. But it's a right windy day."

"Up here it's windy," Lee said. "Should be still

7

enough down below. I'm going on ahead. Hold the horses a mile out. I'll lose off three spaced shots if it's safe to drive them in.''

Sefton was Morgan's top hand. He nodded and Lee toe-touched his stallion's flanks and came down from the pass at a fast clip, dodging rocks, and when the trail was clear he urged the animal to a gallop. The ranch was three miles distant and the stallion covered the ground in minutes.

Lee reined in when he was still five hundred yards out. It would take something heavy, a Sharps Big Fifty or a Remington Rolling Block, to bring him down at five hundred yards, and at that range a shooter would have to be better than good.

There was no wind, no sound except for a red squirrel twittering at the base of a mountain ash; that close to a working ranch there should have been sounds: the cook chopping stove wood or rattling pots, one man calling to another, a door banging open or shut. There should have been something, but there was nothing.

He took the stallion off the trail and walked it out far and wide, circling the ranch buildings. Now and then he stopped and listened. Then he came in from the far side where the pines grew in close and cover was good. He felt a sudden chill when he heard the squawk of buzzards over carrion. He slid the Winchester out of the boot, then getting clear of the pines, he saw what was left of Spade Bit: the main house a burned-out ruin with only the stone chimney still standing. His eyes jumped to the bunkhouse, the cookshack, now piles of blackened rubble. Closer in he saw the dead men, his men sprawled where

8

they had been shot.

McCorkle, the old Scotch cook, lay all twisted up, as if he had died in agony. Old Mac's face was more skull than face, and the buzzards had been at the body. The face and neck and hands had been eaten away, and there were tears in the cook's shirt where the buzzards had gone after the meat of his chest.

Standing still, stunned into immobility for an instant, he watched the buzzards come flapping back again. He raised the Winchester, then let down the hammer: too soon to signal the others to come in. He slapped his hat against his thigh and the buzzards lumbered into awkward flight; gorged with human meat, they didn't go far. They watched him with fierce red eyes as he came forward to check the bodies of the three men he had left to guard the home herd. There was nothing to check: they were nothing but bloated, half-eaten corpses. Next, not wanting to do it, he started to look for the body of his new woman, Maggie. He didn't find it, not in the ruins of the main house, not in the pines where she might have been dragged and outraged.

It was a cool day in the high country, but the stink of rotting bodies was terrible. Guns and gunbelts had been stripped from the bodies of the three men, and even their boots were missing.

The corral was about a hundred yards from the bunkhouse. Past there lay a long stretch of mountain meadow that went over the top of a low ridge and down the other side, good grazing for his horse herd. Sure thing, he thought, except there's no herd left. The corral gate was closed and inside dead horses were everywhere. Here the stink was enough

9

to knock a man down.

Drained of feeling, he went inside and a quick look told him that not all the herd had been destroyed. He made a quick count and stood there trying to make sense of what had happened. They had taken twenty horses, the best of the herd, and slaughtered the rest. Why had they done it like this? It made no sense. Indian trouble was long over in Idaho, but even if the raiders had been Indians, they would have run off every animal on the place. Same for white horse thieves: good horses were big money and this herd had been top quality horseflesh. Not a horse he owned wouldn't have fetched a good price.

He raised the Winchester and squeezed off three spaced shots. There were no ambushers here, no one to be wary of. They were long gone, their bloody work far behind them by now. Not Indians and not horse thieves, he thought, and not some bitter enemy from the past. God knows he had plenty of enemies, yet he didn't think this was the work of somebody that hated him. Somebody that bitter would steal the whole herd or kill the whole herd. It would be one or the other.

The hell with the herd! Where was Maggie? He hadn't wanted to think about her but now he did. Truth was that himself and Maggie didn't get along all that well, but that had nothing to do with the here and now. He didn't love her the way he'd loved his dead wife Sarah, and he knew she didn't love him. What happened was he needed a woman and Maggie wanted to cut loose from the waitressing job in Boise and at the time, two months before, it was a fair enough deal for both of them. In bed she was all

10

a man could ask for, and then some; trouble was they couldn't stay in bed twenty-four hours a day, and when Maggie got up and got dressed she turned into another woman. A fussy, house-proud woman with too many ideas about how the ranch and their lives should be run. But tired of her or not, he would go and search for her. It was something he decided without thinking.

He was walking back to poke through the ruins a second time when he spotted the sheet of paper nailed to a tree. He tore it loose and read what was lettered on it in pencil:

LET ALL TRAITOROUS MORMONS AND GENTILES BEWARE. DEATH AND DESTRUCTION TO ALL WHO OPPOSE THE TRUE MORMON CHURCH ETERNAL DAMNATION TO ALL OUR ENEMIES. IF YOU ARE NOT WITH US YOU ARE AGAINST US. GOD IS ON OUR SIDE AND WILL BRING US VICTORY. THIS IS THE LAND OUR FATHERS FOUGHT AND DIED FOR AND WE COMMAND YOU TO LEAVE IT. REMAIN HERE AND YOU WILL DIE BY THE BULLET OR THE ROPE.

Lee folded the paper and put it in his pocket. The first shock had worn off and now the blood pounded through his body in a killing rage. The Jack Mormons had paid him a visit, renegade Mormons, killer Mormons expelled from the church because they refused to obey the new anti-polygamy laws that made it a crime to have more than one wife. This was Idaho not Utah, and Spade Bit was seventy miles north of the Idaho-Utah border, but he knew about the bloody-handed Jacks. Everybody along the borderline lived in fear of the Jacks and their woman-stealing raids. They needed young "wives" and so they came down from their strongholds in the snow-capped, fog-shrouded mountains and took them, some hardly more than children. Driven by a fierce hatred of Mormons and Gentiles alike, they killed and burned and robbed, and only the young women were spared, to be roped and dragged into the half-explored mountains to the southeast.

That's where Maggie is, he thought, far back in the mountains or on her way there. Now that she was in danger, he was able to think of her with more affection. She had some New England book learning, not as much as she liked to pretend, just enough to make her put on airs, and though he didn't object to the feminine touches she added to the house, there were times when her airs and graces plain got on his nerves. Life on Spade Bit was not to her liking, but she didn't come out and say so. Maggie was too smart for that, knowing full well that if Lee hadn't taken her home with him, ten to one she'd still be waiting tables in that Boise hotel.

Lee heard the new horses coming in from the trail. Sid Sefton rode in first, slid down, looked around with no expression on his face. It took a lot to shake this hard man, but suddenly his face seemed to crumble and he said in a whisper: "Sweet Jesus Christ!" Saying nothing else, he walked over to Lee. His sun-browned face was an ashy color and one eyelid twitched. Lee handed him the sheet of paper without a word. Sefton read it and handed it back.

Lee said quietly, "They killed the boys and took Maggie. They took twenty horses and slaughtered the rest. Guess they couldn't handle more than twenty on the mountain trails."

"Yes," Sefton said. "They hide deep in the mountains."

Bent, Potts and Ford drove in the new stock. Like Sefton, they had been with Lee in the old days. They had stayed on with the new owner, McCormick, when a hoof-and-mouth epidemic killed off the herd and Lee was forced to sell out. They were still there when Lee came back, a long time later, with enough money to buy back Spade Bit, the only place he really wanted to be. He had come back to *this!*

"Jack Mormons did this," Lee said roughly. The three hands were too shocked to say anything. "Quit your gawking and get the new stock up to the meadow. Rope corral will hold them till we clear out the dead animals. Go on now before the stink spooks the animals."

Sefton stayed with Lee. "Never knew the Jacks to raid this far north," he said.

"Must have wore out the border country," Lee said. "It figures they would. Now they're coming north. Greener pastures up this way."

Sefton took a sack of Bull and papers from his vest pocket and rolled a smoke with one hand. The loose-packed cigarette burned fast as he sucked in the acrid smoke. Tobacco smoke helped to kill the stink, but not by much. Sounds of horses and men drifted down from the upper meadow. The sun was

13

warm and Spade Bit had the peace of death.

"What do we do?" Sefton asked. "We start right off maybe we can catch up, rig an ambush."

"No chance of that. They have too much of a head start. Look how far gone the bodies are. Mac and the boys got killed maybe five days ago."

Sefton ground the cigarette stub into the dirt. "Got to do somethin', Lee."

"I'll do something. Just have to figure out what it is. I mean to go it alone, Sid. I don't see there's any other way. Word is there's no way to take the Jack settlement by direct attack. Nobody even knows for sure where it is. I hear tell they're holed up so tight they can't be got at. Guess the army would move on them if there was any chance of winning. You know what happened to that bunch of ranchers and farmers went into the southeast mountains. Was no more than a month after the raiding started."

Sefton nodded. "Read about it in the Boise paper. They got massacred. Fifty went in, two came out."

"That's what I'm saying," Lee said. "Entire party ended up in a box canyon, Jack scouts watching them all the time, didn't have a chance. Two men that escaped were watching their back trail."

Sefton said, "Could be they got massacred 'cause they didn't know what they were doing. Men forget how to fight or maybe they never learned. We're different, we been fightin' all our life. Indians, rustlers, a few times the law. We got a few real good men. You and me and the boys. A fightin' force could be built round that."

"It wouldn't work," Lee told him. He wanted to get on with burying the dead. "I'm not sure a

14

hundred fighting men could get the job done. My guess is there are places in there so narrow only one or two riders can get through at a time. Even if we found the right trail, we'd be single-filed to kingdom come. They could snipe at us, bring down rockslides. Bastards could pick us off from high up, then we'd find them gone if we managed to get up there. Their big advantage is they know that wild country and we don't."

Sefton kicked a chunk of charred wood in helpless anger. "It's a hell of a thing."

"Let it go for now," Lee said.

Ford and Bent rode down and sat their horses, waiting for orders.

"Climb down," Lee told them. "We'll get started with the burying. Out where Buckskin Frank and Catherine are buried. Old Mac and the others were Spade Bit people."

Buckskin Frank Leslie and Catherine Dowd were buried in a grassy clearing back in the pines. Buckskin Frank had gone there first, dying of his wounds after he killed Kid Curry, worst of the Wild Bunch. Catherine Dowd, who loved Frank Leslie all her life, shot a fine horse called Dandy and had the animal buried at the foot of Frank's grave.

"That's some kind of Injun business," one of the older hands said at the time. "Guess she means old Frank to have a good horse in the hereafter."

But he said it in a whisper because no one ever questioned what Catherine Dowd did. Then, some years later, she died too and was buried beside the man she loved.

Ford found a shovel with a fire-blackened blade

and they packed the bodies out to the burying ground and took turns digging the graves. Lee dug Old Mac's grave by himself. McCorkle had been a good old boy as well as a good cook. Old and irritable, racked with arthritis, he worked hard and never complained about anything important. He had been a loyal friend.

"So long, Cookie," Lee said and began to fill in the hole. They got all the graves filled in and stood there in silence. They hadn't wrapped the bodies in blankets because saddle blankets were all they had and they were going to need them. It was as quiet as only a graveyard can be. The wind blew up a bit and rustled the branches of the trees.

"Ain't you goin' to say a few words?" Wesley Ford asked Lee in a plaintive voice.

"No prayers," Lee answered. "You want to pray over them, stay here and do it. Just don't take too long. We got to clear the corral, burn the dead animals."

"Wes," he said to Ford. "Get on down to Zimmerman's Crossing and buy up all the coal oil they got." Zimmerman, a German, kept a general store on the Bridger River about ten miles to the south. He also operated a ferry so he got the travelers coming and going.

Lee gave Ford two fifty dollar gold pieces. "Zimmerman will lend you a wagon on my say-so. Get a water barrel, house building tools, crosscuts, axes, hatchets, plenty of grub. Figure out what we need."

Ford looked puzzled. "What's the barrel for? We got a fine deep well."

Lee turned some of his anger on good-natured

Ford. "Don't talk like a God damned fool. Sons of bitches've probably poisoned it. It'll have to be looked at. You want to drink some, see if it's safe?"

"Not me, boss." Ford ran to his horse and vaulted into the saddle. Nobody smiled because nothing was funny that day.

Thirty-six dead horses had to be burned. Good horses as good as any in the state. A lot of money was tied up in the bloated, stinking carcasses, but Lee wasn't thinking of money. To him the small horse herd had represented a new start in life. Since he was forced to sell out he had battered around North and South America, even the Klondike; and in all that time in Washington State, Mexico, the wild cow country of northern Argentina, there had been only one purpose: to get enough money to start over. Finally the Klondike had brought him luck and he came back full of good feelings and a hunger to make a go of it this time. And now . . .

"Let's get to it," he told the hands. "We'll burn them in six piles. Soon as they're piled we'll cover them with all the brush and deadwood we can find."

He turned to Bud Bent. "Use your machete till Wes gets back with the axes. Fires will have to burn long and hot."

Bent, who had spent time in Mexico, carried a heavy-backed machete in a scabbard behind his saddle-gun. The thick blade was long and sharp without being razor-edged. A razor-edge would dull or gap if you used it for cutting wood. It was different when you swung it at a man's neck.

Lee said, "We'll take the corral apart and stack the posts and rails away from the fire. After that

17

comes the hard part of it."

Sefton spat. Bent and Potts shrugged or grunted. Nobody there was looking forward to roping and dragging dead horses. The dead horses were crawling with maggots and ants; there was the dull buzz of blueflies. But worst of all was the smell.

Stripped to the waist, they worked the rails clear of the posts, then stacked them at a safe distance. Rooting up the posts took longer because they were buried deep. They worked steadily until the entire corral had been taken down and moved away.

Lee told Potts to make a fire and cook a pot of coffee. No one felt much like eating though they had grub—beans, bacon, flour—left over from the horse buying trip. While they drank bitter black coffee, the buzzards, never far away, flapped down for another banquet. Suddenly, Bud Bent, an even-tempered man by nature, jumped to his feet yelling obscenities and started blasting with his six-shot Remington revolver. The hammer clicked three times on empty before he started to reload. He hadn't hit anything.

"Quit it," Lee ordered without getting up. "You're wasting ammunition and making noise. Drink your coffee and never mind the fucking birds. Time to saddle up and get to work."

They worked in pairs: Sefton with Potts, Lee with Bent. Lee pointed to the places where he wanted the carcasses piled. There was no need to tell the men to cinch up tight; they had already done that. It was dirty work but simple enough. The hind legs of the dead animals were roped together before they mounted up and wound the long end of their ropes around steel saddle horns.

The ropes twanged tight and the first carcasses came sliding across the hard-packed dirt. When one was in place, they went back to get another. It put a terrible strain on saddle horns and ropes, but they held, at least for the time being. They had to hold, Lee thought. We have to get this rotten business over with before I can even start thinking about the Jacks and how to rescue Maggie.

He thought about her as he worked. It had always been in the back of her pretty red head that, given time, she could get him to marry her, sell the ranch and then they could move away to another ranch close to some big town. And she would say: "With your energy and experience you'd be an important man in no time. Of course I'm not thinking of myself, not that I wouldn't enjoy being able to entertain nice, respectable ladies and being invited in turn to their homes . . ."

Hours dragged past like a dog with a broken back, and the first three piles were already in place when he called a halt. "Got to water the rest of the horses," he said. "They'll be no good if we don't."

They rode up over the meadow ridge and down to the clear, cold stream that came from the mountain. It was good to wash the sweat off and to drink the sweet water. Then they went back to the job they hated.

Sometime later Lee looked at his old silver-backed stem-winder, his dead father's watch. Wes Ford should be getting back soon if the Jacks hadn't hit

Zimmerman's place. The Jacks could have followed the river north from east Utah knowing beforehand that Zimmerman sold guns. If so, he could kiss the coal oil and other stuff goodbye. But what the hell, even that wouldn't be the end of the world. He would make do; he had done it before. Good water was just over the ridge and there was enough grub and coffee to last a day or two. Brush and deadwood would burn the horses if they fetched enough of it. Doing it that way would take a lot longer, but it could be done.

The sun was on a westward slide and they were still dragging wood to burn the horses. Bud Bent, who had the only cutting blade, stopped the downward swing of his machete. "Wagon coming," he said.

Lee had already heard the rattle of the wagon on the rutted trail. Sure enough it was Wes Ford and they crowded around when he drove in, water sloshing from the poorly fitted barrel-lid. Cans of coal oil were lined up in three rows.

"Got everything you told me to get," Ford told Lee, proud of himself. "Zimmerman was like to piss his pants when I told about the raid. Says he wants the mules and wagon back tomorrow. Could be he's fixin' to pull out."

Lee didn't like Zimmerman, didn't give a damn what he did. For now they had everything they needed and tomorrow the men could throw up a cabin and start clearing the ruins. He wouldn't be there to oversee the work, but Sid Sefton would make sure it was done right. He would ride out at first light, and so far that was the best plan he had in mind. He would head south and see what happened.

The sinking sun threw a red glow over everything and the wind blew hard as it often did at that time of day. "We'll start the burning," Lee told Sefton. "May have to fetch more wood, but now we got the axes to cut it."

There were twenty cans of coal oil, more than enough to get it done. The men waited in silence, knowing that this could be the end of Spade Bit. Lee was a good boss and paid good wages, but there was no guarantee that he could fight his way back from this disaster. They knew—because he made no secret of it—that a good part of the Klondike money had gone into buying back the ranch and the purchase of the first small herd.

"One can to a pile," Lee ordered. "When the fires burn down a bit, soak them again."

Ford came down from the meadow after hobbling and tethering Zimmerman's mules. Lee asked him if he wanted to burn horses or to cook. Ford was a pretty fair cook when he put his head to it, and there had been times when he'd pitched in when old McCorkle was flat on his back with what he called the rheumatics.

He said he'd rather cook and Lee warned him to do it a long way from the horse burning. "If you don't, everything will taste of coal oil."

Sefton was standing by when Lee turned to him. "Everything's wetted down," the tophand said. "No call for you to take part in it. They were your horses."

The night was thick with the smell of coal oil.

"No," Lee said. "I want to light the first match, so I can keep the picture in my head. It'll be a help in the hard times to come. If ever a Jack asks me for mercy I want to remember the men they murdered here, the animals they slaughtered. And then I'll know what to do."

They walked to the corral where Bent and Potts were waiting, their boots wet with coal oil. "Dry them off, for Christ's sake!" Lee said angrily. "Then stay the hell out of the way."

The first wood match flared and he tossed it into the heaped-up brush. Flame boomed up and engulfed everything and the heat was fierce. Lee touched off the next fire and the next and the next. No one said anything because there was absolutely nothing to say.

Far back from the fire, on the other side of the main house, Wes Ford was yelling at them to come and git it.

TWO

Lee was awake long before sunup.

Greasy smoke still curled up from the mounds of burned horses, and it looked like no more burning had to be done. Now it was just a matter of letting the fires burn out and cool before the bones were buried. All signs of the fire would be obliterated by scraping the hard topsoil clean and spreading fresh dirt. The corral would be put back the way it was, then it was best to wait a few days, get rid of the stink, before the new-bought horses were driven down from the meadow.

Pale light glimmered in the east as he walked up to the meadow to look at the fresh stock. Least he had something left. Sefton, who had taken the last watch, could see him well enough, and there was no challenge. Sefton had just come back from checking the herd and now stood by the rope corral, a blanket draped over his shoulder, a .44 caliber Winchester in his hand.

The grass was wet and patches of fog hung in places. It was cold.

"How goes it?" Lee asked, thinking he ought to be on his way but wanting to let the men sleep a little longer. They were bone-tired, had earned their rest. But there were things to be said before he rode out.

"New stock's been restless," Sefton told him. "Quieter now than before. You get much sleep?"

"Enough."

"Me too. You figure out yet what you're going to do?"

"Kind of," Lee said. "If that doesn't work, I'll try something else."

Sefton pulled the blanket tighter around his shoulders. It was as wet as the grass. "Like what?"

They began to walk around the rope corral. Lee said, "There's been talk the Jacks will take in anybody that agrees to convert to their kind of Mormon. Like as not, a few more diehards will join them, misfits or religious fanatics. Probably what they're really looking for are hard cases with gun experience: outlaws, killers, army deserters, the general run of wanted men. You can see how some of them would be tempted to join the heavenly band. A safe place the law can't get at must look sweet. Question is, is it true?"

"It's true."

Lee was surprised. "How the hell do you know?"

Sefton said, "There was an article about it in the Boise paper." Years back some schoolteacher Sefton romanced had taught him to read. Since then he'd been reading everything he got his hands on, especially newspapers.

"Don't believe everything you read in the Boise *Sentinel.*" But Lee hoped Sid and the *Sentinel* had it right.

"Story rang true, the way they wrote it. Man that wrote it, Edgar Upton, stays close to the truth, the way I heard it. Got a reputation to protect and so forth. You fixin' to pass yourself off as a bandit?"

Lee took a cigar from his shirt pocket and put a woodie to it. Darkness was fighting off another day. In the corral the horses were settling down at last, worn out by jittery nerves.

"I might do that," Lee said, savoring the first smoke of the day. "A few years back I used to know a hold-up man and rustler looked something like me. Name of Ben Trask. Same age, give or take a year. Ben was one of Don Luis d'Espana's *pistoleros* same time as me. Drank a lot, talked a lot in the *cantinas.* After Don Luis booted him out for being drunk too often, he tried to get back in the bandit business. *Rurales* caught him half-dead in the desert, hung him from a barrel-organ cactus."

Sefton was testing the top rope of the corral. "Taking his name could get you killed quicker than anything."

"Not too likely. Ben was just a ham and beaner, never an important member of the outlaw fraternity. They'd hardly know him this far north."

"You don't know that for sure." Sefton sounded angry. "How do you know he isn't in the Jack army by this time?"

Lee said, "I know I have to get in there. Anyway, didn't I just tell you he was hung by the mounted police? You're thinking maybe I should just make

25

up a name and a story to go with it. Ben Trask suits me better. I recall how he sounded, how he acted, his little peculiarities. Knowing a man's history makes it easier to take his name, become the man himself."

"Could be," Sefton said reluctantly. "Only thing wrong with it though, which is you can't just ride into the mountains with a sign on your chest saying Howdy folks, I'm Ben Trask, the border bandit, and I'd like to enlist in your devil's brigade. Even if you had some way of identifying yourself, such as false army discharge papers, the Jacks wouldn't buy a pig in a poke. You wouldn't have anybody to vouch for you. You could be anybody, a U.S. marshal, a Pinkerton, an army spy. My friend, the Jacks would kill you out of hand. I was in their shoes, that's what I'd do."

Lee smiled in spite of himself. "Just the same, there has to be some kind of clearinghouse for these law-dodgers, a place where somebody looks them over, takes their measure and sends them ahead or maybe does away with them."

"Does away with them, I'd say. But all right, you get to the Jack fortress or whatever you want to call it. Then what?"

"I don't know, Sid. Getting there comes first."

"This so-called go-between, if there is one, how do you mean to smoke him out?"

"If he's there I'll find him," Lee answered.

Sefton wasn't good at hiding his feelings, which was why he was a poor poker player. Lee knew he was peeved at being left out of this. Now Sefton asked, "You're dead set against my idea for recruiting a war party of men done wrong by the Jacks?"

Lee waved his cigar stub and it glowed red in the gray morning light. "That's right, old friend. Come on, Sid, we got ranch business to discuss."

Sefton wasn't to be put off so easily. "We'll discuss it directly. One last question and I'll button up. Question is, you want me to come with you? No farmer war party, just two so-called law-dodgers 'stead of one. You'd have somebody to watch your back. It would give you an edge you don't have now."

Down below men were rolling out of their blankets. The sound of their voices carried on the still morning air. Time to get going, Lee thought. He liked Sid Sefton but this conversation was going nowhere. He had to set him straight or go on wasting time.

"Look Sid, I need you here. So you're not going unless you want to go by yourself. And that's the end of it. Bud, Charlie and Wes are good men, but they'll work better with you giving the orders. I'm depending on you to look after Spade Bit while I'm gone. There's nobody else. Not too much money left, but I'll give you the best part of it to get the ranch in some kind of shape. Stay on guard. Zimmerman will spread word of the raid, and with me gone it's possible greedy men will believe me dead and the ranch waiting to be grabbed off by anybody tough enough to hang onto it."

Sefton stuck out his jaw, something he did without thinking when he was ready to fight or thinking about it. Lee trusted him as much as any man in the world. "They'd better not try it," Sefton said.

"Watch yourself all the same. Leaving out Old Mac, we're short three men and there's not the wherewithal to replace them. Boise Northwest National has five hundred and sixty dollars on deposit, and that's the end of the money. I'll give you a letter to the manager, but don't go yourself if you run short. Send Wes instead. Conaway, the manager, knows him."

Sefton stared at the horses in the corral. "You sound like you're drawin' up your will?"

"I did that last night by the fire. Just in case, you understand. You never know how things turn out."

Sefton didn't like to hear that. "Tear it up, Lee. Wills bring bad luck."

"Horseshit! If I get killed you and the boys get the ranch. But you'd be in a bad fix without a legal paper to back it up. Come on, leave the horses alone, they're settled enough. I want the men to hear the rest of it. Besides I want my God damned breakfast."

The fires were dying in the smoke-blackened corral, and it still smelled bad, but nothing like the day before. Rain and sun and hard work would return it to normal. Wes Ford was dishing up bacon and biscuits when they got down to the fire. An iron coffee pot bubbled in a bed of coals. Lee and Sefton filled their battered train cups with coffee and they all hunkered down to eat.

"Boys," Lee started off. "I mean to go south and do something about what happened here. Don't talk, just listen. Sid is to be full boss while I'm gone. What he says goes. In spades. If I don't get back in three months, then you'll know I'm dead. That in

28

mind, I made a will last night leaving you all equal shares, but Sid remains boss. That's written in the will. You can sell your share and pull out, but not inside of a year, and you can't sell your share to outsiders. Have to keep it in the family. Naturally you can pull out anytime you like, but if you do it inside of a year, your share stays behind and you get nothing but final wages. That plain enough for you?"

Charlie Potts was offended. "God blast it, Lee, we all been working together for years. Nobody's goin' to make trouble, with you gone." Ford and Bent nodded their agreement. "We'll have the place all fixed up when you get back," Potts finished.

"I'm counting on it," Lee said. "Now finish your breakfast and get to work."

He wasn't sure where he was going and wasn't sure there wouldn't be trouble no matter what Charlie Potts said. Except for their saddles and guns and a few personal possessions, none of the men had owned a thing in their lives. He knew he could count on Sid; the others—well, they were human after all and the thought of becoming property owners might bring a change. Shit! What was he going on about? Bickering, a few fistfights among the men were the least of his problems. Landgrabbers or a return visit from the Jacks—there was real trouble.

Taking a pack animal would make life less of a hardship on the trail, but it didn't fit into the picture of the desperate law-dodger traveling fast and light. He packed a coffee pot and small skillet, coffee, bacon, jerked beef, canned beans. He rolled his blanket and ground sheet in a rubber slicker; the rain could be hard and cold in the mountains. His weapons were a .44 caliber Winchester, one of the new-fangled lever action five-shot Winchester shotguns, a single-action Colt .45.

The lever action shotgun was an interesting weapon that had been introduced by Winchester Arms the year before. He liked weapons and he liked this new shotgun. Winchester sold it mainly to sheriffs and police departments and called it the "alley cleaner." It had been used effectively in prison riots when a lot of fast, heavy lead was called for. Some men said it had some tendency to jam, but it hadn't jammed on him, and he had put it through some hard testing. It worked fine if you bought the best ammunition, and he did.

The men were scraping their plates when he mounted up. They waved, he waved back, and then he was gone. No man would have been able to get him to admit the excitement, but it was there all right, and maybe the quiet, hardworking life didn't suit him as much as he thought. Buckskin Frank, his father, had been like that, always saying he wanted to retire and put the hell-raising and gunfighting behind him and spend the rest of his life raising horses. Except that wasn't easy for a man of his restless nature; if violence and danger didn't catch up fast enough, he went out to meet it. Then came the time, as it did to all gunfighters who can't or won't call it quits, when he met it once too often. Maybe this is my turn, Lee thought calmly, and put it out of his mind.

Pocatello, forty miles distant, was the only town

of any size on the way south, a wild railroad and ore processing center on the Portneuf River near its junction with the Snake. Nowhere as truly wild as the old Kansas cowtowns, it was surely wide-open enough to have a cathouse frequented by local badmen and law-dodgers wanted in some other part of the country, but not in Idaho.

He left the trail before he got to Zimmerman's Crossing—the German would want to gab about the raid—and picked up the river a few miles south. On its way to join the Snake, the river wound through hills thick with larch and pine, and the trail followed its course.

For the first five miles he saw no one; getting closer he passed farm wagons, a few lone riders, a party of Basque shepherds without sheep on their way to town. Lee was in the horse business, so he had nothing against sheepmen. The Basques were a fact of life in Idaho, and all but the meanest, sheep-hating cattlemen had learned to let these dangerous herders alone.

After another hour's ride he could see the smoke of Pocatello far off, then the river made a wide eastern sweep, while the trail branched off and went straight down to the new trestle bridge that ran into Main Street on the other side.

It was about two o'clock when he crossed the bridge; the river below a dirty yellow from the muck the ore plant dumped into it. Smoke from locomotives, their bells clanging, hung over the long, wide expanse of railroad yards east of town. Pocatello was a town of go-getters and civic boosters and there was a new red-brick town hall;

there was even a theater.

A man fitting a new pane to a broken store window told him where he could find a livery stable. "A right turn the next corner, two blocks down from there to Fremont Street, and you'll find a whole slew of 'em. Catling's the best of the lot. Real up to date. Got lockers for you valuables. Padlocks costs you a dollar. You get fifty cents refund when you come back."

He put away his horse and other belongings and went back to Main Street to get a mug of beer and something to eat. The five-stool restaurant provided pork chops, apple sauce, mash and gravy, and when he got through, passing up what was sure to be bad coffee, he went next door to a beat-up saloon with the usual long bar on one side, tables and chairs on the other. Only one man occupied a table, a half-drunk cowhand with a bottle and glass in front of him, his boots testing on a saddle as worn-out as he was.

At that time of day the saloon was quiet except for a handful of men in bib-overalls or canvas work suits. They were talking at the bar or feeding nickels into gaming machines set against the end wall. The three-fruit machines whirred and clanked without paying out any jackpots. A dusty, battered player piano had an out of order sign daubed in black paint. Below the sign some wag had added in pencil: SO IS MY WIFE. Behind the bar a portly bartender walked the duck-boards, collecting empty glasses and beer mugs and dumping them in a zinc trough. Gaboons were placed along the footrail, but most of the spit was on the sawdusted floor. A saloon with

32

no upstairs and no women, it looked like the kind of place it was.

Halfway through the second beer, Lee crooked a finger at the bartender. Change still lay on the bar and Lee pushed a fifty cent piece toward the bartender. "Where they keep the women in this town?" he asked.

"Depends on how much you can spend, mister." The bartender glanced at Lee's soiled wool shirt, thorn scarred leather vest, sweat-stained Stetson. "No offense intended, but you don't look too flush unless you're one of them essentric millionaires you read about in the *Police Gazette.*" The bartender chuckled at his own stale wit. "Mister, I'd say Mrs. Kessler's down by the river'd be about right for you. Kinda rough—got a great big Irish clodhopper for a bouncer—but I would have to say Mrs. Kessler's."

"Mrs. Kessler's down by the river?"

"Just south of the bridge, down a flight of steps and there she is, right where the paddlesteamers tie up. A big old yellow frame house the color of dog vomit, set back from the landing. Tell 'em Eben Claypool sent you. Only don't come back here cryin' if somethin' happens to you. I ain't got no shares in the place."

Looking at the whorehouse from the bottom of the dock steps, Lee gave the bartender full credit for describing it accurately. It was the color of dog puke and probably hadn't been painted since the town was founded. The house was three storeys high, no bullet holes scarred the windows, and that was all that could be said for it. A huge, plug-ugly, check-suited Irishman, who looked like an ape with clothes on, unbolted the door when Lee knocked. Set on the back of his bullet head was a derby a size too small for him. The suit and the derby were yellow, like the house. He looked like an ex-trooper or a railroader turned whore bully. His little pig eyes, rimmed red like a boozer's eyes, regarded Lee with mindless hostility, and given the chance, this roughneck would rather fight than fuck.

"What did ye want?" he growled in a city-Irish brogue. His breath smelled like a week-long poker game.

"A poke," Lee said.

"Oh ye did, did ye? Well let me tell ye somethin', boyo. They'll be none a that durty talk round here. Conduct yerself like a gintleman or take yerself off, do ye get me meanin'? An' ye'll have to check the pistol before goin' upstairs. First rule of the house. Last but not least, no rough stuff or ye'll have me to deal with."

Lee didn't want to give up the Colt but he said all right.

"Ye bet yer balls it's all right," the hooligan said, still wanting to fight. "Payment in advance, no exceptions. What's that ye say? Are the girls clean here? Damn right they's clean. Doc looks 'em over once a month. Never ye mind the girls. Are ye clean yerself? Well for yer own information and eddyfication, ye'll be gettin' a short arm inspection when ye get upstairs. Charges are two dollars for ten minutes and so on. Stay as long as ye like pervided ye behave yerself."

Lee gave the thick mick the Colt and saw it shoved into a pigeon hole behind a wooden counter.

A few other guns were there before his. Then he was ushered into a hot, stuffy parlor with faded flocked wallpaper, a threadbare Turkey carpet, brass-bottomed oil lamps with flowered chimneys, and six whores sitting on two long red sofas. A small, thin woman with a pinched face and a green velvet dress came out of a door marked office and caught a blond, young whore trying to hide a garish dime novel under a cushion. The whore, almost white-blond, got red in the face when the madam glared at her.

"Welcome sir," the madam said to Lee, doing her best to smile. "I am Mrs. Lorena Kessler. I take it Roger has explained the house rules?"

Lee decided Roger didn't look like a Roger and Lorena didn't look like a Lorena. Spike and Lizzie would be more like it. Lee nodded and Mrs. Kessler showed him into her office. He guessed it wouldn't be ladylike to accept poke money in front of the girls.

"Make yourself at home, sir," Mrs. Kessler said. "You'll be with us for how long?"

Lee put a five dollar bill on the desk; already on it were an imitation marble clock, a cashbox, a framed and tinted photograph of a fat man with a handlebar mustache. The fat man was probably the late Mr. Kessler.

"I'll take five dollars worth," Lee said.

"Make it six," Mrs. Kessler said. "For six you get thirty minutes of pleasure. Drinks are available by the bottle or glass. Those six lovely ladies out there are available. Choose the one you like, Mr. . . . ?"

"Ben Trask," Lee said.

"Pleased to meet you, Mr. Trask," the madam

said. "Haven't seen you before, have I?"

Lee knew this old bitch had a mind like a bank examiner: stiff and cold and full of facts. More to the point, he knew some madams curried favor with the local law by turning in wanted men, especially important law-dodgers with a big price on their heads.

"Just passing through," he told her.

He had already chosen the whore he wanted, the full-bodied towhead with a liking for dime novels. Not more than nineteen or twenty, she still had some spirit left. Time would wear her down, but so far she hadn't sunk to the liquor or morphine that kept so many whores going from day to day. He smiled at her and she smiled back, standing up to do her duty by Mrs. Kessler. She had the whitest-blond hair he had ever seen.

"Watch my book, will you?" she said to the whore sitting next to her. "Don't let old Lorena take it."

The other whore yawned behind her hand. "Watch it yourself, darlin'."

Lee's whore took the tattered book with her when they went up to the second floor to a small, narrow room with nothing in it but a double brass bed, a table, chair, wash stand with china jug and basin, a cheap pine wardrobe. An oiled paper shade covered the window and the little room smelled of sweat, lilac water, and sex. On a shelf set high on the wall were a few bottles of scent and face powder.

The whore kicked off her shoes, undid her back buttons with practiced ease, and slipped off her blue silk dress. She hung everything on the back of the chair, then climbed on the bed, opened her legs wide,

36

bounced her backside a few times, and was ready to go to work.

"Come and get it, big boy," she said. "Any way you want it is all right with me. Back or front, makes no difference. You want to suck my thing, there it is waiting for you." Lee was taking off his clothes. "You want me to suck you, just say the word. You've had suck jobs naturally, but tell me this, you ever had a brandy and cream suck?"

"Sounds nourishing," Lee said, his cock standing up straight when he took off his trousers and underpants.

"I find it so," she said. "If you want that you'll notice I don't spit out after you come. Here's how it's done: I take a swig of brandy, a swig of cream but don't swallow before I take you in my mouth. Brandy by itself would be too raw on your member, only the cream cuts it, see. Of course you have to pay a lot extra for a brandy and cream suck. Has to be ordered from downstairs. If that don't tickle your fancy, hows about my special hum suck?"

"How's that?"

"I hum while I'm sucking you and the vibration . . ."

"I take my pleasure the old-fashioned way, me on top of you. After that, we'll see."

"Yep sure fine," the whore said. "The customer is always right 'ceptin when he tries to take his pleasure with a leather belt. Had a kinda old fella try that a few weeks ago. Had to holler for Roger and have his bare ass whupped right out onto the docks. Roger tossed his clothes after him."

"Talkative, ain't you," Lee said with a grin.

A return smile from the whore. "My way of puttin' fellas at their ease. Makes them feel at home, it not bein' so cut and dry. You can call me Towhead if you like. That's what everybody calls me, count of my hair. I'm friendly and you should be glad I'm available. Come on over now. I got to skin you back, make sure you don't give me a dose. Roger calls it a short arm inspection. Army talk, I guess."

She skinned him back and clucked her tongue approvingly. "Clean as a whistle, mister. It'll be a pleasure to do you."

"Call me Ben," Lee told her, positioning himself between her muscular thighs. She had a shaved muff and her love lips glistened with vaseline. He steadied himself with one hand and pushed in right to the hilt. Her muscles tightened and relaxed, while her legs closed around the small of his back. Her hands roamed all over him, stroking his hair, his backside, his tightened-up balls. She bucked her ass and her entire body quivered as he drove in and out of her like a piston rod and soon they were dripping with sweat, soaking the sheets.

Lee didn't realize how wound-up he was until he began to fuck her. This was his first paid-for poke since Maggie came to live at Spade Bit, not that he felt any need to be faithful, and it wasn't because Maggie didn't love him, and even if she had that wouldn't have stopped him if he was away from home and wanted a woman and the need wouldn't wait. It had been none of that. After Sarah was murdered by farmers egged on by the landgrabbing banker Callaway, who swore Spade Bit horses were going to trample their crops, he had buried himself in work, the only way to dull his grief. After Maggie came he had gone on working like a madman, but fucking Maggie as if he'd never get another fuck in his life . . .

"Oh Jesus, you're like a stallion," Towhead whispered in his ear. "It's like you're halfway up my body. That big dingus of yours feels like it can't get enough of me. Christ! I think it's coming out my mouth. That's it, that's it! Bring it right out to the tip, then shove it in—*hard*—all the way."

In and out, in and out, his stroke quickened and he larruped it into her until the brass bed creaked and shook and her fingers dug into his backside and her head rolled from side to side. Her eyes were closed and clean pink tongue stuck out between her teeth. Now her ass bucked so hard that he had to pin her arms to the bed to steady her for his relentless thrust. "Come with me, Ben," she gasped. "Please come with me. Oh my God, I'm coing to come. Come now, Ben. I want to feel your hot come shooting into me."

Her body convulsed and so did his, and he kept on thrusting until he was drained and his cock began to soften, but he didn't pull out, and in a while it grew stif again and they did it again. "You're runnin' up quite a bill," she whispered. "You sure you can pay it?"

"Sure can," Lee said, "and it's worth every penny."

For a whore, Towhead was a great actress, at least in bed, and that was where it counted. Later, after they did it for the third time and he couldn't do it anymore, they lay side by side and talked.

She was an Oregon apple picker's daughter, she said, which might or might not have been true. It was Lee's experience that every whore had a yarn. She was of Swedish descent, she said, which was probably true. Her father and brothers had tried to rape her, had raped her, in fact, so she decided she might as well get paid for getting poked. Her dream was to save enough poke money to open a dressmaking shop in Eugene, Oregon. Men friends, nice customers like Ben, often gave her a little extra to help her on her way.

"I'll be glad to help you," Lee told her.

"How much, Ben? Course you can give me as much or as little as you like. Real nice men have given me as much as fifty dollars."

Lee knew he was taking a chance by asking her if she knew about the law-dodgers that went into the northeast Utah mountains to join the renegade Mormons. But when he asked her, she showed more interest than surprise.

"You mean you're an outlaw, Ben?" she said, sitting up in the sagging bed. "A bandit or a train robber, a real desperado?"

She had her story and he had his. He told her he was from Colorado, had shot a drunken bully in self-defense, but this man had powerful friends and they were out to hang him or jail him for life.

"They'll get me sure if I don't find a place to hide for a while. Man in my home state told me about these outlaws going to Utah to join the Jack Mormons. He was wanted too, for cattle rustling, and he asked me if I knew where these Mormons had their hideout and how to get there. Course I didn't know any more than he did, but it gave me ideas. One last thing this man said was there was some agent or go-between could arrange for a man to join. You ever heard of such a man?"

Now her look was guarded, but she said, "I don't know myself. There might be somebody that does."

"Somebody around here?"

"Maybe right in this house. But listen, I don't want to get mixed up in anything that could get me in trouble. So I can't promise anything, see? I wouldn't mind if you gave me the fifty dollars before I said anything more. Give me the fifty and we could talk more like real friends."

Lee reached over, took fifty dollars from his pants and gave it to her. A little threat was needed, so he made it. "Towhead, darlin', I wouldn't like it if you were telling me tall tales."

That frightened her a little. "Oh no, Ben, I wouldn't do such a thing. We're friends, ain't we. No, this person, this girl I'm talkin' about, is one of the house girls here. She calls herself Nelly Apple-yard, so I guess she is. Tell you the truth, she doesn't belong here at all. Her man friend sold her to Mrs. Kessler, and now she just mopes and cries all the time instead of makin' the best of it. That Clem Haney was worse than an outlaw."

"He *sold* her?"

"Sure he sold her. It's done all the time in this business. But like I said, she can't get used to it. She cries all the time even when Roger doesn't beat her. Oh he doesn't beat her so marks or bruises will show. He used a rubber hot water bottle filled with sand, hits her on top of the head till she goes unconscious. Mrs. Kessler hates her because the regulars shy away from her. No life, no spirit. I guess she even cries when some man tries to poke her. Men have demanded their money back. That doesn't set well with the old bitch downstairs."

"Why don't they just let her go?"

"They got two hundred invested in her."

"But if she's not earning money?"

"They'll kill her anyway, Roger will, some night when he's murderin' drunk. He wants to do it and it'll be an example for the rest of us ladies. Not long ago, one late night, he took her out and held her out over the river at the end of his arms. She came in all white and shaking and threw up on the carpet. You can imagine how Mrs. Kessler took that. I tried talking to her on our day off, told her that brute paddy is going to kill you, you don't get out of the doldrums. I wasn't just talking, Ben. She'll disappear some night and later they'll find her in the river and decide it was suicide, if there's even that much interest. Nobody will give a damn. Women in the Life kill themselves every day. But us ladies here will know that Roger killed her and we'll behave. You're damn right we will. Nobody can do anything about it, not even me, and I like the poor soul."

Lee started to get dressed, but Towhead pulled him back into bed. "Maybe I can help her," Lee said. "I want to talk to her."

Towhead's smile was tired, a little bitter. "You just want information, Ben, or am I wrong. Can you help the poor kid, or is that just talk? Don't get mad. We all got to look after ourselves."

"I want to talk to her. Could be she's got nothing to tell, but I'll help her if I can. Men beating up on women rubs me raw. None of my business, you think. I could make it my business."

On the other side of the wall bedsprings squeaked and there were footsteps in the corridor. Business was picking up as the day wore on toward nightfall.

Towhead raised up in bed and looked at him. "You can't talk to her in my room. Wouldn't be possible anyhow. You start trouble and Mrs. Kessler will tie it to me. I won't let you bring her to my room even if you tell Mrs. Kessler you want her for a three-way. The old bitch will catch on when she thinks about it. She's mean but she's smart. Sorry Ben, I don't want to end up in the dirty river."

This time Lee got out of bed and stayed out. "All right, after I leave you I'll go downstairs and say I want another girl. I'll look the girls over and chose her if she's available. That way there's nothing to connect you."

Towhead got dressed as fast as only a whore can undress. "She'll be available, you bet. Always available is her main problem. You can't miss her: kind of small, pale, with weepy blue eyes. If she isn't available it's because some bastard wants to abuse her. Mrs. Kessler doesn't mind that. But if she isn't there, have a drink and wait. The men that choose her don't keep her long."

Lee pulled on his boots. "Thanks, I'll do what you say. Be seeing you sometime."

"Not likely," Towhead said, "and not here."

THREE

Lee went downstairs and the girl described by Tow-head still sat forlornly at the end of the couch. Some of the whores he'd seen earlier were upstairs with customers. He glanced at all the whores left in the parlor, and some smiled, some yawned, and then he settled his bill with Mrs. Kessler. The madam put the money in the cashbox and said, "Thank you, sir, and please call again."

"I'd like another girl," Lee said.

"Oh." Mrs. Kessler raised her eyebrows. "Didn't you like the young lady you had?"

Lee winked. "Liked her fine. But now I'd like to try something else. Lately I been in places they got few women of any kind and would like to make up for lost time."

Mrs. Kessler was pleased to find such a pleasant, prompt-paying customer. "Well why not? You're a healthy young man. I can see that. They're out there waiting for you. This time there's no need to pay in advance. Pay when you're ready to leave."

The whores whispered and giggled when they realized he was going to pick a new poke. Nelly Appleyard looked up at him, then back at the floor. Her face was pale and drawn and there were dark smudges under her eyes. One of the whores burst out laughing when he stopped in front of the Appleyard girl and said, "Let's get acquainted, missy."

There was more laughing and Mrs. Kessler came out of the office looking mean. "What's the laughing about?" she demanded to know.

Frightened, the laughing whore said, "This gentleman just picked Nelly. Oughtn't of laughed, I guess."

"But you found it funny?"

The whore squirmed under Mrs. Kessler's dark, mean eye. "Guess I'm feeling silly today."

"I'll talk to you later, Angelica," the madam threatened, turning to Lee. "You may find this young lady a little shy."

Lee went into his country shitkicker act. "I like all kinda ladies, God bless 'em."

Towhead came downstairs and took her place on the sofa, and for all the notice she took of Lee, she might never have seen him before.

"Go along now, Nelly," the madam said. Nelly Appleyard went with Lee, and some of the whores giggled in spite of themselves. Mrs. Kessler told them to be quiet or they'd know the reason why.

Going upstairs the girl stumbled and Lee kept her from falling. She mumbled her thanks and he told her to think nothing of it. Her room was on the third floor.

"No call to be scared of me," Lee said, opening the door she pointed to. "Nobody's going to hurt you."

Once inside, not looking at him, she began to fumble with her buttons. Lee said, "You don't have to do that." He kept his voice low. "All I want is to talk to you."

He sat her down on the chair and he took the bed, facing her. It could all be a waste of time. The thug who deserted her, actually sold her into whoredom, could have told her anything or nothing.

"What do you want, mister?" Her thin voice was made thinner by despair.

Nothing was to be gained by dragging it out. "I want to know where Clem Haney went after he left here?" But you never knew about women: she still might have a soft spot for the son of a bitch. "I'm no kind of law, no kind of hired killer gunning for your man. Where did he go?"

"He's not my man, not anymore." Her voice was so faint that he could barely hear it. "I don't what you want, mister. What's he got to do with you?"

Lee told her he was a wanted man trying to hook up with the Jack Mormons only he hadn't been able to do it. Big money could be made if he joined the Jacks. Better than that, he'd be safe from the law, which would stop looking for him if he stayed out of sight for a year or two. The look on her face told him no further explanation was needed.

Not being beaten or threatened gave her a little courage. "How'd you hear about Clem?"

"Clem told a fella that told me. Us law-dodgers gossip like old women, like for instance such and such a fellow robbed a train with three other fellas.

46

Such and such a fella got hung, got shot. Or the talk could be about a fat bank waiting to be robbed. Or what big rancher is hiring on gunslingers. Business talk, you could say. Where did he go? I can help you, make it worth your while."

Nelly Appleyard reached over to take a towel from the washstand, dipped in the water jug and pressed it against her forehead.

Though she was young, about twenty-four, her face was haggard, as if she had given up hope. Not much given to pity, Lee pitied this forlorn woman.

But he had to push her because she was so scared of everything. "I *can* help you, Nelly, if you tell me where Clem Háney's gone to. I know he's gone to be vetted by the Jack Mormon agent. Clem liked to talk, is my information. He must have told you where this agent is located. Tell me and I'll take you out of here, stake you to a train ticket and enough money to keep you going till you get a job—whatever."

She looked at him with teary eyes. "Clem said nothing, he just left. Look mister, whoever you are, can't you see I can't help you? I don't want to get in worse trouble then I'm in. I'm nothing but a greasy whore in a whorehouse. If you want a poke or a suck, there's the bed."

Lee still hoped to break her down, no matter how hopeless and bitter she was. For an instant there had been a faint look of hope in her eyes, and then it was gone, driven out by fear and mistrust. She wanted to believe him, but her misery got in the way.

Kindness hadn't worked, so he decided to be

47

brutal. "All right, girlie, you don't trust me because you don't trust me because you don't know me. How about the Irishman and the old hag downstairs? You ought to know them well enough by now. You know that vicious bastard will kill you sooner or later. Get on his bad side once too often and he'll murder you. He broke you in, am I right? The whore bully always breaks the new girls in no matter how many men they've been with. His way of putting his stamp on them. But that's nothing compared to what he'll do when the killing mood is on him. He'll throw you in the river when he's tired kicking and beating. If he hasn't beaten you senseless, you'll be glad to drown. You want to take some time to think it over?"

She nodded, he said nothing.

It was getting dark and Lee stood up to light the handing lamp. He trimmed the wick and put the chimney back in place. A paddleboat hooted on the river. Nelly Appleyard had her eyes closed, her hands clenched tight in her lap. Finally she spoke.

"How can you get me past Roger? You don't even have a gun."

"Never mind the gun. I'll get it back. What kind of gun does Roger carry?"

"A big, heavy gun with a short barrel. Sometimes I see him with his coat off. The gun is in a holster under his arm."

Could be a Colt .45 with a cut-down barrel, Lee thought. Or a breaktop five-shot .455 British Webley, a stubby gun with a hell of a wallop. Could even be a Colt Lightning double-action .38 To a woman a double-action .38 might look bigger than it was.

"What if there's nothing to tell?"

Lee was getting sick of her. "You got plenty to tell. Make up your mind. You're scared Roger will come after us, after you after I get you out. Not a chance. I'll cripple the son of a bitch so bad he won't be able to walk to the shithouse. I'll put him on crutches for the rest of his life. One more time: where did Haney go?"

"Eutaw Springs. He went to Eutaw Springs to meet a man named John Spargo who runs a trading post." The words came out in a rush, as if she couldn't say them fast enough. "That's the truth, I swear it. Clem said this man Spargo was the one who decided who joines the Mormons, who doesn't. Clem bragged about how they'd be happy to take on a big man like him."

Lee thought: And if they aren't glad, if Spargo isn't pleased with what he sees, all Clem will get is a bullet in the head and a deep grave. Because that was certain to be the way they handled it, so there would be nobody around to talk about it. Recruits were sent on ahead or they disappeared. No loose ends. It made good sense from where the Jacks stood.

Talking seemed to calm her a little, though she continued to dart nervous glances at the door, afraid the Irishman would come crashing through at any moment. She stopped talking and he waited.

She said, "I'm just telling you what Clem told me. You can't blame me if he told me a lie."

"I'll chance it."

"Clem says it's not even a town. He said Spargo's saloon and trading post is all there is. You ever heard of the place?"

Lee knew she was talking to cover her fear, to put off having to go downstairs to face the whore bully's gun and maybe die in front of it. Panic would take hold of her again if they didn't go soon.

"It's time to leave," he told her. "I'll go down first, you'll be right behind me. I'll settle up with Mrs. Kessler and start to leave. Take your place on the sofa and don't move till I yell come ahead. Don't get scared if there's a lot of noise out where Roger sits. Get out fast no matter what I'm doing. Get out and wait close-by. I'll be right behind you, that's a promise. If not, get to the train station as fast as you can."

He handed her fifty dollars, enough to take her far from Pocatello. "Just don't panic," he said.

The office door was open and Mrs. Kessler was talking to a runty man who was twisting a silk hat in his hands. Lee said he was leaving and wanted to settle up. The runty man went out ahead of Lee. Mrs. Kessler closed the door.

Lee went out through the archway that led to the front door where the Irishman sat on a stool by a peephole. The Irishman took a swig from a flat pint bottle before he eased his wide backside off the stool. He didn't like Lee and maybe he hated the whole world because he was nothing but a drunken whore bully and knew it and didn't like it. Now he was slightly drunk.

"You was upstairs a long time, wasn't you? Had

trouble gettin' it up, haw? Ye can tell ol' Roger. Might be able to give ye the benefit of me wide experience with women."

Lee knew he had taken on a load of whiskey, but he talked without slurring and his movements were steady. Booze wouldn't slow him down all that much.

"Some other time," Lee said calmly. "I'll take my gun."

"Certainly sor, Yes indeedy sor." He guffawed. "Take care ye don't shoot yerself in the foot, sor. T'would break me heart, ye did yerself an injury."

Laughing to himself he went behind the counter where the checked guns were kept in wooden pigeon-holes. He put Lee's Colt on the counter and folded his arms. More than ever he looked like an ape with clothes on.

Lee picked up the Colt and said, "You made a mistake, mister. This isn't my gun. My gun is a brand-new Remington .44. Take another look and you'll find it. Or you want me to call Mrs. Kessler and have this straightened out?"

A darker shade of red colored the Irishman's booze-mottled face. He roared like an injuried bull. "What the hell are ye tryin' to pull. Ye gave in an old Bisley Colt, ye got back an old Bisley Colt." He unfounded his arms and leaned forward, hands flat on the counter. "Now get the hell out of here before I get cross."

Lee swung the heavy pistol and smashed the Irishman on the head just above the forehead. He swung up and down and hit the Irishman in the same place. A short, savage chop broke the Irish-

51

man's nose and blood spatterred like rain. Another man would have dropped like a stone, but the Irishman stayed on his feet, fumbling for his shoulder holster. His Webley .455 was coming out cocked when Lee brought the Colt down like a club and broke the Irishman's wrist. The cocked double-action clattered to the floor and fired as the hammer came down and the Irishman scrambled to grab it up with his good hand. Lee hit him twice on the back of the neck and his face hit the floor and he lay still.

"Come ahead, Nelly!" Lee yelled. "Nelly, come ahead!" In the parlor the whores were screaming, running for the stairs, calling for Mrs. Kessler. Lee shouted again, then vaulted over the counter and kicked the Irishman in the side of the head. There was nothing personal in the way he shattered the Irishman's leg bones by stomping on them until he felt them grinding under his boots. For good measure, he kicked the Irishman's kneecaps loose. He jumped over the counter and saw Nelly running down the hall. He grabbed her by the hand and pulled her after him. A gun fired behind them and a bullet ripped into the front door and he turned and saw Mrs. Kessler steadying a double-barreled derringer for a better shot. He put a bullet close to her head and she ducked out of sight.

A paddlesteamer with only one light showing was moored at the landing; it was quiet up and down the dark river. If anybody heard the shooting, they hadn't come running to see what it was about. He helped her up the steps to the bridge, where Main Street began and naphtha lights flared white in the darkness. A town with so many saloons was late getting to bed and there was considerable traffic in the street and on the bridge. No city policemen were in sight.

The girl was trembling all over. Lee tightened his grip on her arm and told her to take it easy. "Nobody's coming after us. Take my arm and walk slow like we're out for an evening stroll. It's only ten o'clock. Go slow, I said. Talk, smile, you can manage to do that."

"Yes," she said.

On the next corner a city policeman stood shifting his weight from one foot to the other. Going past they got more and more than the usual bored look policemen give people, and then the bridge and the whorehouse were far behind and the girl stopped shaking and trying to look over her shoulder.

Then her questions came in a string, as if she had been saving them. "What if Mrs. Kessler sets the law on us?" Mrs. Kessler stayed very much on her mind. So did the Irishman. "Is Roger dead? Did you kill him? If he dies will we be sent to prison for a long time? Why should I be sent to prison? He was a very bad man."

Lee said Roger wasn't dead and the law wouldn't be coming after them. "You were sold like a slave and kept as a slave. There's nothing to worry about. Mrs. Kessler won't go near the police. How can she? The police want nothing to do with Mrs. Kessler or her place. Mrs. Kessler will see doctoring Roger as a business expense or else she'll throw him out and get herself another bully. Forget all that. Where do you want to go?"

"I have to think," she said.

All along Main Street the saloons racketed with life musicians, player pianos, mechanical harps. Pocatello was a mixture of the old and the new. Horses were hitched under the new-fangled naptha streetlights, and there were signs advertising painless dentists, Eagle Lock typewriters and horn gramophones. On the second floor, in a commercial block, a chiropractor advertised his services with a pair of giant hands manipulating a gigantic spine. It would take more than a chiropractor to put Roger together again.

"I want to be on the first train out," she decided.

"To where?" Lee asked her. "The ticket agent will want to know that."

"The first train, any train. I wish you were coming with me."

Lee didn't want to get into that. "You'll be all right as soon as you board the train. But he wasn't sure this weak-willed woman would ever be all right. She would take up with some other glib bastard and it would be like that for the rest of her life. In the end, it had nothing to do with him.

He put her on a train for Salt Lake City and went back to get his horse. Time to be gone before Mrs. Kessler rounded up a bunch of thugs and put them on the streets asking questions about a tall man and a pale lady.

Clear of the town, he rode south on the road that crossed the Idaho-Utah line and went straight down to Ogden and then to Salt Lake. Northeast of Ogden were the mountains where the Jacks were holed up, or so it was said. According to Clem Haney, if you could believe anything he said, Eutaw Springs was in the foothills that ran up into the western slope of the Rockies. The Jacks had the Rockies at their backs, no way to get at them there. But he wasn't betting that the Jacks hadn't found and mapped an escape route, even if it meant climbing up into the peaks and down the far side. The original Mormons had been some of the bravest, most daring explorers in the world; this bunch of renegade bastards came from the same venturesome stock.

But for now there was nothing to do but find out if Eutaw Springs existed. It wouldn't be on any maps. He would stay on the road until he was about ten miles north of Logan, then swing east and cut along the south end of Bear Lake, the biggest lake in northeast Utah. Past the lake, he would have to feel his way.

Once he reached the Idaho-Utah line, he would have to watch his step. This was country that had suffered Jack raids and naturally people would be suspicious or everybody and anybody. In normal times, a lone rider wouldn't be seen as any special threat. Nowadays a lone rider could be an advance scout for a Jack raid. Any inquiries he made, at this ranch or that, would have to be made in the full light of day, which was no guarantee that he wouldn't be shot from ambush by a jittery rancher before he got close enough to ask questions.

A good road and a bright moon made travel easy. Close to the Utah desert, it hardly ever rained in southern Idaho. He would be about eighty miles from Spade Bit when he reached the borderline. Long before now the boys would have fixed up the corral and started clearing the ruins. Tomorrow or the next day they get started on the cabin. He hoped to see Spade Bit again.

He stopped to drink water and to splash some in his face. He had gone more than twenty-four hours without sleep. Times past he could have gone longer than that, but helping to drag and burn thirty-six dead horses was back-breaking work, and the few hours restless sleep he got the night before had done nothing to rest him. Sleep, what he got of it, hadn't come easily, and there were nightmares that brought sweat in spite of the cold mountain air. Towhead and the bed-tussle had released most of the tension, and his hot hatred of the Jacks had cooled to the point where he could control it. A man who couldn't control himself was a likely candidate for killing. A man didn't have much of a chance when hate governed his every move. Yet the hate was there, and it would stay with him for the rest of his life. In this, he was very much like his father, who never found it possible to stop hating a man because he was dead. Once, talking of a man he had tracked down and killed, Frank said, "I wish I could restore him to life so I could kill him again."

Tiredness was making him groggy. East from the road he would find a place to unspool his blankets after he watered his horse and put the animal on a long tether so it could graze. He was hungry, but not hungry enough to risk a campfire in this country; morning would be time enough to cook coffee and fry bacon.

On both sides of the line the country looked much the same and it took a look at his watch to let him know he had to be in Utah by now. For all his travel-

56

ing, he didn't know this part of the country, though it was less than a hundred miles from Spade Bit. He yawned. God damn, it would be good to sleep.

He wondered how Maggie was faring. For somebody with such "respectable" notions, it was a hell of a fix to be in. He yawned a bone-cracking yawn. What the hell did respectability mean? If respectability meant turning into a mealymouth psalm singer and tightwad, then he wanted no part of it, and he sure as hell wasn't about to get married again, least all to Maggie, who could only get worse once the knot was tied. There had been hints, of course, dozens of them, but he had turned a deaf ear when the subject came up. Maybe it was time to stake Maggie to a new start and send her packing. If I get her back, if we live through this, that's what he'd do. He would miss her in bed, but the world was full of women and he would find someone to take her place.

Trying to remember everything he knew about Ben Trask didn't do much to keep him awake. Ben was originally from Colorado and though he claimed to be from Texas he didn't have the slow Texas drawl, which was all to the good because Lee knew he was no kind of playactor. One way or another, it was nothing to fret about. Except for the famous badmen, most small-potato outlaws and gunslingers told so many stories about their past lives that nobody gave a damn.

He came to the trail that went east from the Logan road. It was rutted by wagon wheels and probably went east to the Mormon farms on the flat side of Bear Lake. It should take him to the lake and then he would ride south to get around it.

Here, off the road, there were no farmhouses, no lights far back in the bare brown hills. Moving on, he spotted a stand of scrubby trees with a shallow creek on the far side of it. Past the trees the creek made a bend and lost itself in stunted hills. Under the trees, protected by shade, was enough grass for his horse.

He saw to the animal, unspooled his bedroll and fell into a deep, dreamless sleep, with his hand resting on the lever action shotgun.

FOUR

When he rolled out in the morning, he could see the mountains to the east. Far back were the peaks vaulting into the sky. Set against the cloudless blue sky, the peaks looked jagged and flatsided, like the painted scenery he'd seen in theaters.

He cooked a big breakfast and as he moved on the country began to change; the arid country fell behind. Mountains closed in as he rode, but they were nothing like the mountains on the far side of Bear Lake. These were real mountains, the granddaddy of all mountains, the Rockies, and the Jacks were in there somewhere, far back and high up, thinking themselves secure from any attack.

By afternoon, he figured he was about halfway to the lake. Bear Lake was a big lake; how big he didn't know; it might take a while to get around it. Not a patient man by nature, he could be patient when he had to. The Jacks wouldn't run away, and neither would Maggie, and whether she liked it or not, she would have to suffer along with the other captive women. She would have been raped many times by now, for the Jacks were a horny bunch, but it wouldn't kill her. It might make her hysterical, as old Mac the cook used to say; poor Maggie, with her airs and graces, should have stayed in Massachusetts.

Lee was watering the stallion from his hat when the three farmers came out of the brush. Big rocks were scattered through the brush, and they had been in there, watching him. He heard them coming before they showed themselves. If they had wanted to kill him from cover, they could have done it long before they started making so much noise.

Most farmers couldn't shoot for beans, but with three men shooting at him from a rest position, at least one bullet would have found its mark.

He turned to face them, careful to keep his hand away from his gun. The two older men were bearded; the young one had a week's black stubble on his face. They looked like farmers, but you never knew; a closer look at their weapons told him they were just farmers. The Jacks had the money to buy better weapons. The older men carried breech-loading, single-shot Army Springfields, worn and battered and probably bought from some traveling gun dealer. The young farmer had a Big Fifty Sharps, the buffalo gun. All wore farmer clothes, black and dusty.

Lee looked at their weapons. "Don't have a lot of money," he said. "Ninety-seven dollars and an old silver watch. Take what you want. It's not worth dying for."

60

The young farmer, not much more than twenty, took a tighter grip on the Sharps. "What the hell are you talkin' about, mister? You think we're road agents?"

"You mean you're not?"

"He thinks we're road agents," the young farmer said. He had a high voice and his laugh was high-pitched. "Don't that beat all."

"That'll do," one of the bearded men ordered. "Nothing funny about it. What're you doin' here, mister?"

Lee looked at the rocks sticking up out of the brush. They might have left their best shot back there, ready to drop him if he made a wrong move. They might be smart enough to do that.

"Who wants to know?" Lee asked. "Is this a private trail, or what? You got something against strangers?"

"Depends," the bearded man answered. "Depends on what kind of a stranger you might be. You have the look of a gunman to me."

"You said it right, Jacob. He sure looks like a gunman." This was from the third man, who hadn't said anything. "Ask him what his business is. Ask him what he wants."

Lee didn't know why the man couldn't ask his own questions. But he left it to Jacob, who seemed to be leader of this threadbare outfit.

It came out that the others were Paxton and Ike.

"You better speak the truth," Ike warned. Ike was the youngster. Lee knew he was ready to use the Sharps, maybe wanted to use it. Young Ike was a farmer, but he had the makings of a killer; people

61

might be talking about him in a few years. Ike wanted to catch him in a lie, or what he decided was a lie. It would be hell drawing against a cocked Sharps.

Lee told them he was Ben Trask from up in Idaho and was searching for his sister, Isabel. Ike started to say something, but was shushed by Jacob. "Isabel took up with a drifter that figured to marry into her share of the ranch. Wasn't no share, but he didn't know that. If she had a share it would become his property. So he thought. Guess she told him— lied about it—to keep him interested. I ran him off with a shotgun, but he came back by night and took her with him. Iz was always wild, always kicking the traces. They could be married by now, but I mean to take her back a widow. I hope to find her in Laketown."

Ike gave out with his shrill laugh. "You don't believe in young love, mister?"

Jacob said angrily, "Shut your mouth, let him talk." He spoke like the others except for a slight foreign accent.

"It's all bullshit," Ike jeered. "You got eyes, you can see this fella don't own no ranch. Look how he's got up. Don't even have a clean shirt. He owns a ranch, why don't he have riders to back him?"

Jacob was quiet in contrast to the babbling kid, and he had clear, gray intelligent eyes: a Bible reading German or Scandinavian. Lee knew the solemn farmer would kill him if he thought he had to, or he would try, and if he succeeded he would speak some appropriate verses over the grave.

"Boy has a point," he said. "You got no men siding now."

"My sister is family business. Not right to drag hired hands into a family quarrel. I look after my own in my own way. You look like a man would understand that. What's this about anyway?"

"What it's about is Jack Mormons and you could be a gunman fixin' to join up with them. You don't know the Jacks been raidin' along the border of your state?"

"Sure I know. Bad news travels. It was in the papers. What've Jacks got to do with me? I told you I was looking for my sister."

Ike whinnied. "More likely his runaway wife, his so-called wife. Maybe his runaway grandmaw. He's lying, I tell you. What say we lay a rope across his back. That'll get him to talk in a hurry."

Jacob paid him no heed. "You say your sister's in Laketown. Why there? There's nothing there. A one-sided street, is all. How'd you get Laketown in your head?"

Lee said, "My sister mentioned this fella's father had a ranch around there. She was mad at me, said they could go there if I wanted to be mean about the marriage."

Jacob didn't frown, didn't do anything. "That can't be, mister. Ain't no ranches down that way. Some farms. It's farmin' country. Maybe your sister didn't get it right?"

"I don't know," Lee said. "She said a ranch."

"A chicken ranch," Ike sneered. "Five thousand head of Rhode Island Reds. Down there they got to wear snowshoes so's not to be hip-deep in chicken-shit."

Jacob put an edge in his voice. "Hold your tongue, boy. What's your sister's fella's name?"

"He said he was Andy Jackson Belford. Came by my place with a busted leg. Said a rattler spooked his horse. I let him have a spare bunk with the hands till the leg mended. My sister Isabel fussed over him, swallowed his lying stories, finally decided she wanted to marry him. Not entirely her fault. It can get lonely for a woman up there."

It could go any way, Lee knew. Finally it would be Jacob who made the decision.

"You tell it straight enough," Jacob said deliberately. "Or you could be a champeen liar. I got to think a minute."

Ike cut in with, "He's lying. Every word he's sayin' is a lie. Look him over good. He's nothin' but a saddlebum gunman lookin' for work. That fine horse don't belong to him. He stole it."

The stallion was grazing on sun-dried grass about fifty feet away. Lee called the animal and it raised its head and came to him. Lee scratched the animal between the ears and it whinnied, wanting to get back to grazing. A word from Lee sent it away.

"It's your animal sure enough," Jacob admitted. "That don't prove your story. You got anything to prove your name? Old bill of sale with your name on it? Tax akcessment? A piece of paper of that nature?"

Lee pretended to get mad, not mad enough to get shot for it, just mad enough to show he had some guts. "You know a law says a man has to prove who

64

he is? Carry documents and papers like they do back in Europe. My grandfather used to say a man had to carry them or get locked up. You sound like maybe you came from over there, mister. I'm surprised you'd want to start that horseshit in a free country."

Jacob squared his shoulders, looked pretty peeved. "I'm as good an American as you. Maybe better."

"Making a point," Lee said. "No offense intended."

Jacob relented. "None taken."

"Then what's the verdict? Listen to me a minute. You better listen, mister. I'm resting my animal, minding my own business, and you people come out of the bushes like bushwhackers and I'm supposed to tell my whole history. What gives you the God damned right?"

Jacob was wavering, wanting better proof that Lee's story was true. Ike wanted to kill him. Not too bright, Paxton just listened to what was being said.

Jacob said in his slow voice, "We got to be extra careful, don't you see? It's been hell and damnation down this way. Was a time a man could ride these roads and not a finger would be raised to him. Now that's all changed, with no man trustin' another without he knows he knows him real well. We got to stop ever'body comes into this country. You sound like a decent white man, only there's a big hole in your story. Which is, how come we didn't see your sister and this man you say she's with?"

Lee shrugged. "Maybe she lied to throw me off. They don't have to be in Laketown."

"You said they was," Ike cut in. "You said that."

Lee shook his head. "I said they could be in Laketown, close to there. I meant to take a look, ask questions. Then look someplace else if I came up dry."

Ike gave out with his womanish laugh. "You wouldn't come up dry on a chicken ranch. Maybe your brother-in-law's old man raises hogs as well as chickens."

Keeping his temper, which was real enough, Lee spoke to Jacob. "You tell sonny here to watch his mouth or I'll shove that buffalo gun up his shithole. What kind of man are you, letting a man be bad-mouthed with your gun on him?"

Ike took a step forward before Jacob ordered him back with an angry shout. "Stay back, I told you. You want me to send you back to the farm? I'll do it you don't stop jawin' like the fool you are."

Jacob stared at Lee. "I think you better turn about and go back. Your sister, this man, wasn't through here. They'd a-been stopped. This road is watched night and day. I'd a'heard about it one way or another. We can't let you go on. Every gunman throws in with the Jacks is one more miserable thing we got to deal with. That's how it is, the situation bein' what it is. Go back."

Lee's voice was hard and flat. "Nobody turns me around on a public road. You want to kill me, then do it. You want to commit murder, here I stand. Tell you one thing, mister. I get out of this I'll put the law on you, swear out a complaint."

Jacob stood his ground; he was a tough old bird.

66

"Swear out all the complaints you like, Sheriff knows where to find me. Go on back."

Lee knew the other man was ready to yield. A lifetime of law and order still had its hold on him. "I won't do it," Lee said. "Only way to stop me is to kill me."

Ike said quickly, "Let me kill him. You're so holy-joe, you don't have to do it. I'll even do the buryin', you don't want to dirty your hands."

Jacob swung the old Springfield toward Ike. "You shoot this man I'll shoot you. The both of you get back in the brush. You got wax in your ears, or what?"

Jacob's voice rose to a shout and Ike slouched away, trailed by Paxton.

Jacob turned to Lee. "You still fixin' to set the law on me?" His attempt at a smile was pretty poor. "Don't mind it if you do. It's your right. Wish there was some law around here. Send the sheriff if you like. He'll come. It's safer than takin' on the Jacks."

"Forget the sheriff," Lee said, liking the old farmer. "You been having a bad time of it, I can see that."

Jacob said mournfully, "Not much we can do about it except watch the roads. We turn back some, but that's not to say they don't get past by cuttin' acrost country. Or they come down from north of Bear Lake and get into the mountains from there. Wild country north of the Lake."

Lee whistled for his horse. "I'll be going."

Jacob looked after him.

The sun was gone and the road sloped down and

he saw the scatter of lights that was Garden City, the dull shine of the big lake beyond it. He circled the town, not wanting another set-to with nervous, suspicious locals, and got back on the road a few miles south of it.

High up, the road followed the lake except where a rockface cut down into the water, and in places like that the road climbed higher, but where it was possible, the road stayed with the lake.

After a while the mountains fell back from the lake and there was a long, wide stretch of green country, good farming country, that ran dead ahead until it was lost in darkness. Far back from the road were the lights of a few farmhouses. They might be showing lights, he thought, but there were men with guns waiting in the dark. Men taking the first watch as soon as night closed in.

A dog barked and far away another dog replied. A pale moon drifted behind massed black clouds. No one challenged him and he made good traveling time.

Late that night, even with a clouded moon, there was enough light to see Laketown's one-sided street set high above the lake. The lake was fed by rivers and creeks and melted snow from the mountains, and the town was set high above the shore so spring floods wouldn't wash it away. Only one light showed, and if Laketown had some kind of law, that was probably it. Now came the part he didn't like, asking about John Spargo. There might be nothing to it if Spargo wasn't under suspicion—in this country a man didn't have to do much to be suspected of something—but he had to go down and ask, else he could be wandering for days. If trouble waited down there, he couldn't duck it by just asking where Eutaw Springs was. Clem Haney said there was nothing there but Spargo's trading post and saloon, Spargo himself, and maybe a woman and a hired man.

Smart thing—maybe—would be to go right to the town law, probably a marshal, and ask him; asking a bartender or storekeeper came to the same thing: the marshal would know in minutes and there would be questions as to what this stranger was doing in nervous country that got few strangers.

He decided to stay with the story of the flighty sister, because Jacob might be having second thoughts along about now. There was a chance he might follow along to see how the search was going.

But there was no trouble with the marshal, none at all. Old and stiff at sixty or so, most likely he'd been in the job for twenty-five or thirty years. Settled farming country, where there were no ranches, no sheepherding, seldom new serious trouble and Marshal Purdy Boykin—his name was on a faded sign beside the jail door—must have led a nice full uneventful life before the Jacks came. Trouble was the last thing he wanted with anybody.

Lee slept for four hours and was up early. Still too early to go down into town. From high up, screened by brush, he watched the town and the road coming from the north. Nobody came or went. On the far side of the lake, its flat gray surface reflecting the morning light, were the foothills, the bottom rung of the mountains that rose higher and higher to become fog-shrouded peaks. Now and then he

69

caught a glimpse of the peaks through drifting clouds. It was cold where he was, but it was colder up there, where the snow stayed all year, and it looked like it was raining.

The town began to wake up. Cookstove smoke spiraled up from chimneys' a man came out onto a porch and pitched a basin of slop-water into the street; a blacksmith started pounding iron.

Lee led his horse down through the brush, then mounted up and rode into town. No one was in the street when he got there and knocked on the nail-studded door of the marshal's office. Down the street he heard a window being pushed up. He knocked again and a crabby voice told him to hold his hosses.

A dead-bolt scraped back and the door opened a crack. A lined gray face with gray stubble and wire-rimmed glasses on it looked out at him.

"What? What's it you want?" Marshal Purdy Boykin wanted to know. His voice quavered as if he expected to get a bullet for an answer.

Lee said, "Sorry to bother you so early, sir, but you're the man I got to see. My sister Isabel ran off with a man . . ."

The door opened most of the way and Lee saw an elderly man in a red flannel undershirt blinking at him. The hot smells of coffee and bacon drifted out.

"All right, come in," the marshal said grudgingly. "You say your sister run off with a man. Run off, wasn't abducted. Well now, how does that concern the law, here or anywhere? But take a chair, why don't you, and I'll listen to what you got to say."

The marshall put on a shirt and hat and sat behind

a battered oak desk. He buttoned two buttons of the shirt, but didn't tuck it into his pants. His tarnished badge was pinned to the left pocket of the shirt. The pot-bellied stove glowed red and the office was hot and smelly. Close to the stove, on a table with a sheet metal top, stood an old iron coffee pot and an equally old fry pan with bacon and sliced potatoes in it.

"Don't let me keep you from your breakfast," Lee said.

On the wall behind the desk a sheaf of yellowed reward posters hung from a spike. The poster in front had a police—or prison-made photograph—of some oldtimer wanted for stagecoach robbery. Lee couldn't make out the date of the crime, but it couldn't have been recent.

"I will eat, you don't mind," the marshal said. He filled a coffee cup and ate his bacon and fries straight from the pan. He had good manners and didn't talk with his mouth full. When he got through, he said, "You can't be from around there or I'd know you. Same would hold for your sister."

Lee said, "We're from up in Idaho. Man she ran off with is a rascal and I aim to take her back."

The marshal had little interest in flighty sisters, but he felt he had to ask, "What would bring them here? This town is as dead as Kelcy's Nuts. You saw for yourself what it's like. You sure you got the right place?"

Lee said he had the name of the town right. "I didn't expect to find them in town. This rascal that enticed my sister said he was going to talk business with a man named of John Spargo runs a trading

71

post at a place called Eutaw Springs. Ever hear of it or him?"

"I know him," he said laconically. "Not well, just by sight. Though I haven't laid eyes on him in—I don't know—three or four months. Comes to town now and then he needs something he don't stock at the post."

At least he exists, Lee thought. Spargo was a living, breathing human being and not the invention of some law-dodger's whiskeyed imagination.

"Glad I didn't come this far for nothing," Lee said.

"Don't be too glad. Wasn't no report of a strange woman passin' through here with a man or by herself." Then the marshal checked himself, thinking maybe he was getting into something he wanted to stay out of. "Course they could have got to Spargo's place by a different route. Or they could have come through late at night. People do come through at night, not many, a few. I can't see every blessed thing that goes on, can I?"

"A man has to sleep seven or eight out of the twenty-four."

"Right you are, young man. As for getting to the Springs, it's a good piece from here, east of the lake, far back in the foothills. Sounds like a town or settlement, but it ain't. Just Young John Spargo, son of Old John Spargo, and his trading post and saloon. Old John started the business in the late Thirties before the trappers killed off the fur animals. Still some trapping can be done in the mountains—animals are coming back—but you got to work hard to do it. Trapping or no trapping, Young John, as he's called, hangs on there. Must make some money with the post and saloon. Course Old John was pretty well fixed by the time he died."

"You been there?"

"Not in years," the marshal said. "Had to go lookin' for a man that murdered his wife—caught her layin' down for this brother—and took to the mountains. Couldn't find him, it was winter. Come spring we found him froze to death. That was one tough search, I can tell you. Course I was a lot younger. That was thirty years ago and ain't been to the Springs since then. But I ain't finished tellin' you how to get there. County road, a rough trail up the east side of the lake. You'll pass a few farms, then nothin' north of there. Up the middle of the lake it gets to be real bad country not fit for nothin'. Stay on the lake trail till you come to a worse trail goin' east into the hills."

"I'll find it," Lee said.

"You will after I finish tellin' you," the marshal said irritably. "Take that trail—there's about fifteen miles of it—and you'll come to Spargo's place smack-dab against the foot of the mountains. Can't miss it. It'll be lookin' right at you."

Lee thanked the marshal and started to leave. At the door he turned and said, "One last thing, marshal. On the way in here from the Logan road three farmers held rifles on me, wanted to know if I was on my way to join these Jack Mormons I been hearing about. I thought the Jacks were way west, in the mountains north of the Great Salt Lake. You got Jacks around here?"

The marshal drank coffee just to be doing something. "I don't know anything about no Jack Mormons," he said after straring into his cup for a good fifteen seconds. "They may be sheriff's business or territorial business or army business, but they ain't my business. I'm strictly a town marshal. If there are Jacks in these parts, and I'm not saying there are, they don't bother the town and they don't bother me. We like to have it like that."

So that was it. Laketown and the marshal had struck some sort of arrangement with the Jacks. Maybe it hadn't been talked, but a deal had been made. As long as the Jacks didn't burn them out, the townspeople and the marshal saw nothing, heard nothing. That was why the marshal hadn't asked questions, why nobody ran to gawk at him as he rode in.

"Close the door as you go," the marshal said before returning to the rest of the breakfast.

A few people looked at Lee as he mounted up. Nobody said "Mornin'," nobody did anything but look and quickly look away.

He had been saving the stallion for this last stretch of country. Now he urged the big animal to a gallop when he saw the first of the farms the marshal had mentioned. It was well back from the road, with trees planted north of it to break the wind. He guessed most of the farmers in the lake country were Mormons, but a few Gentiles would have moved in to farm since the government forced the Mormon leaders to open the Utah Territory to settlement. But Mormon or Gentile, the farmers along here, like the townspeople, had made some kind of deal with the Jacks, otherwise they would

74

have been burned out. This wasn't so unusual when he thought about it. For one reason or another, badmen of one kind or another, often held back from raiding too close to home.

Two hours later he was clear of farm country. Here the trail got very bad and it had few signs of use. At times there were long stretches of rocky broken country between him and the lake. The trail dipped and climbed, but mostly it climbed, and the hilly country on that side of the lake was covered with sagebrush and greasewood and occasional patches of pinon pine.

The trail grew narrower as he went inland from the lake, and soon he was high up enough to be able to look back at the lake, though he couldn't see the western shore because fog had settled in during the late afternoon. There was fog on the lake and heavier, wetter fog up ahead and it began to rain, and when it showed no sign of letting up, he unrolled the slicker and put it on. The long loose skirts of the slicker kept his saddle and weapons dry. So close to the mountains, the rain was very cold, and it beat down as if it meant to go on forever.

He was hungry and to dull his hunger he smoked a cigar, shielding it against the rain, but it got wet anyway and he threw it away. He had hoped to make Spargo's place by nightfall, but there was no chance of that.

The trail continued to wind up into the hills. Later the rain turned to drizzle and that stopped and everything dripped. He knew he risked getting shot if he ventured into Spargo's place after dark, and it would be dark and late when he got there.

It was close to dark, and raining again, when he came to a fork in the trail with a signpost standing beside it. SPARGO was lettered on the flatboard, and that was all. This was where Spargo land began, or where the original John Spargo decided it began. Back in the Thirties, even before the Mormons came, there would be no one to dispute his claim, and now, more than fifty years later, this country had no more value than it had then. He still had fifteen miles to go, no use even trying to get there before morning, so he used the last of the light finding a place to spend the night: a deep, brushy hollow off the trail, with plenty of leftover rainwater for the stallion to drink and the sparse grass there would have to do.

He draped the rubber ground sheet over a bush and crawled in under it wearing the slicker. Building a fire, even a small one, was dangerous. Under the slicker his clothes were damp. Using the saddle as a pillow, he managed to sleep.

It rained several times, but he stayed dry enough.

FIVE

Next morning, in gray light, he was saddling the stallion when two men rode by, heading for Spargo's place or the mountains. They didn't see him because the light was thick and there was some mist and he was in good cover. The two riders were up high and outlined against the eastern light. Not that he got much of a look. They were riding hard and were gone in seconds, but he figured he'd know them again. Sure as hell they weren't farmers or lawmen or they would have used more caution. They could be Jack scouts returning from a mission; any renegade outfit, any fighting outfit, was only as good as the information it gathered. Yet, from the look of them, he figured they were law-dodgers hoping to get the nod from Spargo. Didn't much matter what they were unless they were chasing him.

He gave them thirty minutes start, let them get well ahead, before he mounted up and moved on. Later he topped a ridge and there was a bowl shaped valley below. He dismounted, climbed up the safe side of a big rock, and used binoculars to look for places where he might be bushwhacked. If they were waiting, he didn't spot them.

He rode with the Winchester in one hand, the reins in the other. The stallion was well trained, but horses were just plain dumb no matter how many tricks they learned, and a sudden burst of gunfire could throw the animal into a blind panic that could kill or cripple both of them.

He eased his way down the slope and started across. Down below floodwater covered the trail and he walked the stallion through it, waiting for rifles to crack. But nothing happened and halfway across the trail came out of the water and it began to climb and there were plenty of places where they could be stretched out with their rifles pointing at him. Still nothing happened.

Out of the little valley, past places where an ambush could hardly fail if they knew their business, he decided they had nothing to do with him. Just the same, experienced ambushers sometimes picked unlikely places, so now and then he reined in and scouted the country ahead before he went on. The sign he picked up from the trail told him they were still traveling fast.

Spargo's place, when he finally saw it, was located at the base of a high, smooth rockface that sloped out at the top to make an overhang that protected it from the wind and weather. The main building looked like three log cabins joined together many years in the past, and it was tarred against damp rot. There were two outbuildings and a big, solid stable, and a crapper stood back in the pines. Pines grew in close except where they had been cleared in front to make a big wagonyard. The spring, circled by willows, was at the base of the cliff. It bubbled up at the bottom of the cliff and the overflow created a small pool that in turn spilled over and was lost in sandy soil. A big weathered sign above the main building stated: JOHN SPARGO & SON/SALOON & TRADING POST/FURS BOUGHT OR TRADED/SUPPLIES SOLD.

Lee didn't spot a lookout, but he knew one was there. One of the outbuildings faced the trail and the man sitting in shadow stood up and gave a shout that brought two men hurrying from the main building. The lookout didn't show himself, stayed where he was. Lee knew he'd be shot out of the saddle if he did anything.

One of the men who faced him was short and barrel-chested and wore a thick untrimmed beard. Lee figured that was Spargo. He was dressed in rusty black, coat and trousers, and he wore a round-crowned, preacherish hat and a dirty white shirt without a collar. He had a heavy pistol in a plain black holster and he had his hand on the butt. The other man, old and stooped and dressed in ragged buckskins, carried an old 15-shot Henry rifle, nicked and scratched by hard use, but otherwise well kept. Like Spargo, he was bearded, but his beard was far from virile and hung down from his emaciated face in dirty, lifeless strands. Lee could hear his mumbling: a loony.

Behind the two men, framed in the doorway, was a young girl with cropped hair, wool shirt and worn

79

Levis. Lee couldn't get a good look at her. He waited while Spargo looked him over. He took his time, then said, "Who are you, mister, and what brings you here?"

Coming from his beer keg chest his voice sounded as a bear might sound if a bear could talk. The matted black beard grew so high on his face that it looked like he was wearing a mask.

"I'm looking for John Spargo," Lee answered. "I have business with him."

"You're looking at him," Spargo said. "What do you think your business is? Say it short and sweet."

"Word's out you're looking for men. I want to hire out my gun to the Jacks. You said keep it short."

The girl had moved forward in the doorway. She had short brown hair, a heart-shaped face, copper-studded, and she wasn't as young as he'd first thought. The rubber-handled Colt .38, the Officer's Model with the swing-out cylinder, looked too big for her, even when belted high as it was.

"Never heard of them," Spargo growled. His rumbling voice carried without effort.

The old man gave a crazy laugh.

Spargo said, "I run a saloon and trading post and nothing but. Still you're here so come on in so we can talk. Just leave the animal, it'll be looked after."

The girl stepped aside to let them in. She was mad about something or else her face had a naturally sour look. Spargo gestured for Lee to go first and he went into a big, wide, low-ceilinged, smoky room with a rough plank bar—boards laid across very old whiskey barrels—and a scatter of tables and chairs.

The two men Lee had seen on the trail that

morning now sat at a table with bottles and glasses in front of them. They looked at him with no particular interest. Both were in their middle-thirties, wore range clothes, cartridge-studded gun-belts, and looked like the law-dodgers they were. A third man not with the other two stood in the center of the room with his hand on his beltgun. Spargo told him to sit down and he went back to his table and picked up his glass with his left hand, still looking at Lee.

Spargo jerked his thumb toward a table at the end of the bar, set well away from the others. He wasn't friendly or unfriendly; his flat, rumbling voice didn't give anything away, and there was nothing particularly violent about him. But Lee knew that he was about as dangerous as a man can get.

"We'll be more private here," he rumbled.

The old man sat at one of the tables with the brass-framed old rifle across his lap. The girl stood by the door with her hip stuck, her hand resting on the butt of the high-holstered .38. One of the men Lee knew from the trail took out a deck of greasy cards and began to deal to himself. Lee wondered if Clem Haney had been here and where he was now. Only two things were possible: he was buried deep or in the mountains with the Jacks.

Spargo put a bottle and glass on the table and sat down. "How'd you hear about this place?" He watched as Lee poured a trickle of whiskey. He wants to see if I drink too much, Lee decided.

Spargo wore brass shirt studs instead of buttons and he hadn't washed himself or his shirt in a dog's age. "Keep it simple," he advised Lee.

"I'll do that," Lee said.

"Wait." Spargo turned as the card dealer threw the cards down, lurched over to the girl and whispered something. There was a slap and a hard push and the law-dodger's spurs dug into the floor and he crashed down on his back. He was red-faced and cursing and reaching for his gun when the girl's gun came out fast and already cocked.

"Try it," she said.

The old man cackled and Spargo slapped the table with the flat of his hand. "Quit it!" he bellowed. "You there, card shuffler, pick yourself up and go back where you was. Do it now."

The floored badman went back to his table, slopped whiskey into his glass, tossed it off. His partner leaned across the table and tugged at his shirt sleeve.

"You done good, Missy," the old man said to the girl.

It got quiet again and Spargo said to Lee, "You was about to say how you heard of this place. Keep it short now."

Lee said, "An army deserter told me. Happened in a saloon in Leadville, Colorado."

Spargo's face registered nothing. "He just up and told you he was a deserter. You just met the man, so you say, and all the same he told you he was on the run. Why would he do that?"

Lee knew Spargo was just stringing him out. No way any of it could be checked. Spargo watched his face intently, as if he thought he could read the truth there.

"He was footless drunk," Lee went on. "Said he

was on the run from Fort Sherman and knew there was a place he could hide and never be found and make money at the same time. Being hunted myself, I asked where this place was. He got crafty and winked and changed the conversation. I figures he was busting to tell me—tell somebody—and when I said it didn't matter a damn he still kept silent, but after more whiskey he got loud and cantankerous. Who the hell was I to doubt his word, and so forth? Then he came right out and said he was going north to join the Jack Mormons."

Lee couldn't see much of Spargo's dark eyes, but he sensed resentment. "They don't like to be called that, mister." There was a pause. "That's what I hear. Go on."

"I told this drunk I never heard of these Mormons —who were they? He told me in dribs and drabs, holding things and then letting them out the drunker he got. A mishmash of a story, but he was so convinced he got me convinced. I asked him how he planned to join these people? If they were raiding and killing and all the rest of it, why would they trust a stranger? A few drinks later he told me about this place."

Spargo said, "He mention me by name?"

"No. That he absolutely couldn't tell me. A big secret. You know how drunks are. I figured he didn't know. But he did say there was a Mormon agent in Eutaw Springs, Utah, who passed on everybody that wanted to join up. Guess that would be you, Mr. Spargo."

"You guess wrong. This deserter, he say how he heard of Eutaw Springs?"

"Not in so many words. I didn't press it too hard or he would've got huffy about it. Mostly he talked like he knew things other people didn't know. Conclusion I came to was he just heard rumors he wanted to believe."

Spargo stared at Lee. "And you come all this way on the word of a loudmouth drunk?"

"I figured there might be some truth to the story. It was worth taking a chance. What did I have to lose? I needed a place where I could lay low for a while."

Still staring, Spargo said. "What you do to make the law so determined?" He scratched this thick of beard every time he asked a question. "Shoot the Governor of Colorado?"

Lee wondered why Spargo was hedging so much. He knew he'd be killed, anyway they'd try, if his story sounded fishy. Maybe Spargo was one of those men who can't say anything straight.

Lee said, "I killed two men while I was stealing horses belonged to the Circle X in West Texas. A big outfit. One of them was the owner's son. Man has political pull so the law's working harder than usual."

Spargo scratched his dirty beard. "You say the law knows you come north?"

"No. I rode clear across Kansas with nobody following along. On the prairie you know if somebody is behind unless they're an Indian tracker. I think I'm in the clear for now."

Spargo growled, "I wouldn't like it if the Texas law, any law, followed you here. You say not, but I don't know that. We'll let that go for now. A word of caution: don't get cocky. Here your guarantees don't mean a thing."

Spargo scratched his beard. "You have to kill those two men? Or was you just havin' fun?"

"They came at me from nowhere, in the dark. There was enough light for them to see me. I shot the both of them, then got in close and shot them on the ground."

"You don't look like a killer. Which don't mean you ain't killed a man or two. There's a difference though."

"Never claimed to be a killer," Lee said. "They could've killed or wounded me, brought me down, got me hung. What do you think, Mr. Spargo?"

"About you?" Spargo stroked his beard when he wasn't scratching it. Messing with his beard was what fist-pounding and arm-waving were to preachers and politicians. It kept him busy all the time. "I don't know what I think about you. Haven't made up my mind."

Lee knocked over his chair getting up. He threw a silver dollar on the table. "I'll be on my way. Looks like I came here for nothing."

Spargo didn't move. "You ain't going no place, sonny. Sit down and keep your temper."

Lee remained standing. Here was where he'd find out for sure. "Who's to stop me?"

"Me, I'll stop you. Me and him—and her." He meant the old man and the girl. "Don't let his age fool you. A word from me and he'll put five bullets in you so fast you won't even know you're dying. Sit down. I'll decide when I'm good and ready."

Lee sat down. "How long do I wait?"

"Didn't I just tell you? You wasn't invited here or drug here. You come on your own free will. You're here and here you stay till I decide. Getting me mad won't help your case. Clear?"

"As day," Lee said.

"Good." Spargo stood up. "I like men that see the sense of things when they're explained. Now sir, we got a few rules here has to be followed. No wandering off, might get lost. No mixing in with the other men. Keep your distance. Like for instance you wouldn't want to get friendly with a man turned out to be a wrong 'un. No card playing for fear of fights and gunplay. The man that pulls a gun in here, less he's pushed, will get shot. Had two men had a gun dispute a while back. Now they're not here."

"You'll have no trouble with me, Mr. Spargo."

"I knew you was a right-thinkin' man." Spargo lowered his voice even more. "That man over there that bothered the girl. Now that was a fool thing to do, cause it's obvious she waint no whore. That man for what he done is down in my black book and as for yourself don't think sweet-talkin' will work where grabbin' didn't. Try that and you'll have me after you not to mention the old man. His granddaughter there is the apple of his eye."

Lee glanced at the girl and she glared back at him. "I'm not that dumb. It wouldn't be worth it."

"It would if you got away with it." Spargo never smiled. "You're tired and want to sleep, bunks are in there." He nodded to a door. "Want food, the girl will fix it for you. We got beef and venison and smoked ham. Only I got to tell you everythin' cost more than you'd pay in a reg'lar restaurant."

"You want to see green?" Lee asked. "I got about a hundred dollars."

Spargo glanced at Lee's money. "That should cover it. You didn't have to say how much. I'd a-trusted you for it."

Sure you would, Lee thought. I have a fine stallion and a saddle that cost two hundred dollars.

"Everything here is for sale except the girl," Spargo said. "But should Missy take a fancy to you, well then that's her business. But put it out of your mind, it ain't goin' to happen. If you don't want to bunk in with the other men and listen to them snoring, there's some cubicles with doors so a man can sleep in peace. Good value for the money."

"Suits me," Lee agreed. "Can you have the girl fry me up a steak and cook a pot of coffee. What number cubicle?"

"Only three cubicles, ain't got numbers, take your pick. Grub'll be ready in a minute. You go ahead."

Spargo spoke to the girl called Missy and she went into the lean-to kitchen built into the side of the house. In there she slammed things around. Lee waited while coffee and steak smells came out of the kitchen.

The law-dodger who'd been shamed by the girl was putting away liquor at a good rate. Some of the whiskey slopped on the table, dripped to the floor. The sullen outlaw's partner kept on trying to settle him down, but it didn't do any good because now he wanted to beat up the girl more than he wanted to poke her. He scowled at the old man, then at the kitchen, and kept drinking. Spargo had gone into

87

the other side of the building, probably where the supplies were stored. That law-dodger's going to get himself killed, Lee decided. And his partner, if he butts in, is going to share the same grave.

The girl strode across the room with the food tray. Her face was flushed and sweat beaded her upper lip. It looked like she was hopping mad all the time. She slammed down the coffee pot and steak platter.

"You want sugar for the coffee?" She threw out the question like a challenge.

Lee shook his head. "How much?"

That made her angrier. "You settle with Spargo. I'm not waitress."

Lee took the whiskey and the food into one of the so-called cubicles. A narrow space had been partioned off against the back wall of the bunk room. Two cubicles had rickety doors and the third hidey-hole he looked at wasn't as beat-up as the others. It was about the size of a jail cell in a mean jail. The bunk room smelled bad, the cubicles a little less so. No table, no chair, nothing but a plank bed with a thin mattress and a torn blanket. It would do.

He propped himself against the wall and started on the steak. He was reaching down to take the coffee pot off the floor when there was a knock. He eased his gun in its holster and called out, "Come in."

It was the girl and she held out tin salt and pepper shakers. "You forgot these," she said. "I salted and peppered the meat. Some people like it saltier."

"It's fine as it is." It wasn't all right, it was too God damned salty, but he didn't say that. He noticed the she closed the door when she came in.

She stood there doing nothing. Her face was sun and wind burned and her light eyes were even lighter against the reddish tone of her skin. A small, good-looking woman about thirty, or a few years past it. The rough life had aged and lined her a bit, but she would have been welcome in any man's bed. Her shirt was too big for her, but her breasts filled it out.

She still hadn't said anything.

Lee said, "Maybe I could use more salt and pepper," and felt like a fool after he said it. Soon he'd be saying things such as "Nice weather for this time of year."

She came close enough to hand him the shakers. Their hands touched and she drew back, but didn't leave. She stood with one hip thrust forward, something she did without thinking, and he felt a stirring in his pants. He crossed his legs but she was on to him.

She said, "Spargo says you call yourself Ben Trask."

"It's my true name. What's yours?"

"Missy. Missy Landry. It's French. That's my grandfather out there. His grandfather came from France. You ever been to France."

"Never have. How about you?"

It was the wrong thing to say. She flared up. "You know God damned well I never been to France. Who are you to poke fun at me?"

"Nobody. I wasn't poking fun."

"I been to Salt Lake though. My grandmother was born there and wanted to see it before she died. We spent ten days there and she died there. I came back here and been here ever since. You ever been to

Salt Lake?"

"Never got the chance," Lee said.

"At least that's one place you haven't been," she said.

The steak was terrible with even more salt added to it. "Lots of places I ain't been to."

"My grandmother taught me to never say 'ain't.' It's not good English. My grandmother could read from beginning to end, didn't have to puzzle out the words."

Lee drank some coffee, which wasn't any better than the steak. "What happened to your mother and father? Just asking?"

"You can ask," she said. "They left and never came back. That was when I was eight. Maybe they died or maybe they didn't want me. My grandmother raised me, taught me to read. She's been dead for sixteen years."

"You like it here?"

She didn't like the question and her sudden, fierce look said so. Lee noticed that her hand always came to rest on the butt of her gun when she got mad, he way of telling the world that she wasn't going to take any shit from anybody.

Lee decided the coffee wasn't as bad as the steak. The man who got this girl was going to get a rotten cook. "You don't have to tell me a thing," he said.

She frowned at him. "I've got nothing to hide. I wouldn't mind leaving here. Sparago knows that. Years ago, when I was a kid, he thought we should get married. I said no and he dropped it. Now he's getting old and has settled into his own rut. Same with me. My grandfather can't live forever and when he dies I'll have to leave. It's leave or stay here for the rest of my life. Spargo says he'll leave me his money if I stay."

Lee shrugged. "You'll think of something."

"I'm thinking about Spargo's money," she went on. "Grandfather says he has some put away and I'll have that. How much he won't say. I'd leave now if he'd go with me. Except he won't. Nothing could drag him away from these mountains. He was here before Spargo's father. A long time. Says he's the last of the mountain men. I guess he is. All the others are dead. He knows these mountains up and down, backward and forward."

The old man must be the guide, Lee thought. Spargo sizes up the outlaws and the old man takes them in if they pass the test. How the girl fitted in he had no way of knowing. But it was likely, the old man being so old, that she would go along too.

He wondered if she had ever been with a man. Many men must have tried, but that gun on her hip and the old man always around, she might still be a virgin. Lee didn't know if he'd ever had a rassle with a virgin. They said you could tell, but he wasn't so sure about that.

Looking at her and feeling like it, he was ready to risk a brief ride in the hay. Spargo said what Missy did was her business. He was so matter of fact about it that he probably didn't care. But you never knew. There was the 15-shot Henry to think about. The hell with the old man and his ancient Henry. You took your chances when you wanted something badly enough.

But nothing happened.

"Mr. Trask . . . Ben," she said with some hesitation. "I think you like me because you have a bone in your pants for me. I'm used to rough talk, so don't mind me. You'd like to do it with me and I with you. But not here, not with those men out there. Later, maybe. Would you like to poke me when I'm more prepared for it?"

Did she mean some night on the mountain? It would be better in a bed, but he'd take it any way he could get it.

"I'd like that very much," he said honestly. He didn't ask what she meant by "later." He didn't ask because he knew she was saying things she'd never said to any man. He thought he knew. And of course he could be as wrong about her as the lunatic up in Bridger County who jumped off a bluff was about his homemade wings.

"I'll be going now," she said.

Right after she left he heard somebody guffawing in the saloon. The laughter was loud and forced and ill-natured. The ugly tone was unmistakable even coming as it was from a distance. Then he heard Spargo's rumbling voice and it got quiet. A door slammed.

Lee went out and Spargo and Missy weren't there, then he spotted them through the windows, walking away from the house. They went out of sight. Lee turned to go back to his hidey-hole.

"Jackass braying woke up, did it?" the old man asked in his toothless, crazy voice. His own laugh was more of a wheeze. He laughed until tears ran out of his faded blue eyes. "Next time the jackass does that throw him a fork of hay."

Lee ignored him, turned to go. Behind the woman-shamed drunk outlaw said, "The old man's got a real big mouth, but you got nothin' a-tall to say. Now why is that? It ain't sociable that you won't let on how she is. Is she a good poke or just fair to middlin'? Is she loose or is she tight, so on and so forth?"

He sounded very drunk and Lee wanted no truck with him. He half-turned, not enough to get back-shot. He knew the drunk was going to push it no matter what he did or said. The third man, sitting by himself, took his bottle and glass and went into the bunk room. No sign of Spargo or the girl: they are having a long confab.

The first hard push came. "How was she?" the drunk said. "Does she suck cocks? Matter of interest, y'unnerstan'."

"What's that you say?" The 15-shot Henry came up off the table. The old man had been mumbling. Now he was silent. "You talkin' about my grand-daughter, you dumb jackass son of a poxy hoor. I'm goin' to stop your mouth for good."

The drunk was too drunk to be afraid of the rifle. Or else he thought the old man wouldn't shoot without Spargo's say-so. That's what he thought. He said, "You ain't goin' to kill nobody. You ain't goin' to risk your meal ticket killin' without orders."

"I'll be told quick enough. You wait." The old man backed out holding the rifle. "Young John comes back you'll whistle a different tune. Draggin' my little girl's name in the shit bucket."

The door slammed and Lee was left with the two outlaws. Their gun-rigs marked them for gunslingers and he didn't doubt they were fast enough. He knew the drunk would get to it in a minute. No way to head it off, no way to duck it. Spargo, unless he happened to be close-by, wouldn't get there in time to stop it.

The drunk's partner said something, but the drunk stood up anyway and was quick enough for a man with half a bottle in him. "I ask you is the women a good poke. You don't say nothin'. You think you got a crotch claim on the woman. Like hell! You don't look like you could poke your mother!"

Lee just looked at him. The other man got up and moved back from the table. Lee knew he was fixing to knock over the table and use it as a shield if this turned into a gun battle. Saloon fights often did. The drunk grinned when he heard his partner move.

"You can stay out of this," Lee said.

"Got to side my brother," the other man said, sounding tired as if he'd backed his loudmouth brother in too many stupid fights.

Outside there was a yell and the drunk went for his gun. It came out fast with the hammer going back when Lee drew and shot the drunk's brother in the chest. He was sober so he got it first. He took the bullet through the lung and still managed to pull his gun before he staggered and fell forward on his face. His gun fired into the floor. The drunk got off a shot and missed. Lee shot him twice while he was still earing back the hammer for a second shot. He sagged and folded and fell. On the floor his dying brother was still clawing for his gun. Lee took aim and shot both men in the head. Spargo came bulling through the door with his gun in his hand.

Lee stayed where he was. Spargo came across the room with the old man behind him. The girl had her .38 drawn. Spargo said, "Drop it, mister."

Lee held his Colt dangle by his side. "Don't crowd me, Spargo. They asked for it and they got it. That right, Mr. Landry?"

"Mr. Landry!" The old man was startled. "*Mister* Landry! He's tellin' the truth, Young John. They come down hard on this fella, the drunkard did. Forced him to a fight."

Spargo let down the hammer and holstered his gun. So did the girl. The old man stooped over the bodies, stepping in blood. He scuffed his blood-wet boots in the sawdust.

"Couldn't be deader," he announced.

"You and Lem get rid of them," Spargo told the old man. "Trask, you sit down."

Lee sat at Spargo's table by the end of the bar. Spargo got coffee from the kitchen, asked Lee if he wanted whiskey.

"Had enough," Lee said.

"That man you killed had too much. I watched the whole thing through the window. Could have stopped it, but wanted to make sure if you could handle it. I'd already decided to get rid of them, send them back. The quiet one had somethin' to him, but the drunkard—was his brother—would have got him into trouble. Did get him into trouble one last time."

"Then you know I didn't start it?"

"The old man told me. I saw it for myself."

"Does that mean I'm all right with you?"

"I guess so," Spargo said. "But from here on in, when I tell you to do somethin' you do it. I told you to shake the gun and you didn't."

"I thought you were fixing to kill me," Lee said. "I thought I'd kill you while you were killing me."

Spargo waved the matter aside. "Probably I'd have done the same. Forget it. There's more important things to talk about. Missy and the old man will take you in. It's a long, hard journey and some of it is walkin'. Expect some blisters, my friend. A bit late in the season for real heavy snow, but nature don't run like a train schedule. You could get a light fall, you could get ten feet. Don't start bellyaching if there's snow four feet over your head."

"I'll manage," Lee said.

Spargo frowned. "Don't interrupt. And don't downgrade the old man and the girl. They can go places you wouldn't think possible. In the mountains the old man especially is like a goat. Go all day, go all night if he has to. Listen hard to what I'm going to tell you next. Which is you can't join the Jacks and then decide the life doesn't suit you and you want to go home. Can't be done. You know too much by then. No exceptions. Nobody leaves—ever."

"I hear you," Lee said.

"Oh sure. It's easy to say yes," Spargo said. "Easy to say yes here in a room with a good steak under your belt and prob'ly feelin' cocky cause you just dropped two men. I know you're feelin'. Fine with me, how you feel. Here you ride out anytime as long as you pay me for room and board. We shake hands and it's been nice to make you acquaintance.

With the Jacks that don't work. Go against orders and it's the end of you. They tell you to kill your brother you've got to do it. They're like an army in there. Only one general, everybody else is soldiers. You got any doubts, now's the time to lay them on the table."

"No doubts," Lee told him. "I'm ready to go any time."

"All right then," Spargo said. "You leave first thing in the morning. You know what I like about you, mister? You don't ask too many questions. Most men in your place would've."

More probing: Spargo never stopped. "Would you have answered them?"

"Hell no, not hard questions. I don't know. Could be you'll like it in there. Good food, good accomodations, no shortage of women. Only don't go jumpin' women you ain't supposed to. They hang you for that."

Under the cliff it got darker faster than out in the open, and the room was full of shadows when Spargo got up to light a brass lamp that stood on a shelf behind the bar. The smell of gunsmoke remained and so did the smell of death.

"Don't be expectin' the old man or the girl," Spargo said. "They got their own cabin. I sleep in there." That was the supply part of the building. "Me and them will be taking turns on the watch during the night. You got enough liquor in there? Be sure now. I wouldn't want you stumblin' about in the dark. Use the chamberpot you get the call of nature. Don't go outside."

"I get your meaning," Lee said.

"Sure you do," Spargo said. "Now I would think this is a good time for you to go to bed."

Spargo followed Lee into the bunk room where the lone man lay snoring. He didn't just blow out the light there, he took it with him.

Lee took off his boots and stretched out on the bed. Except for Spargo's light the house was in darkness.

SIX

They started into the mountains after Missy cooked a big breakfast—hamsteaks, pancakes, biscuits, canned peaches, coffee—that the old man said would have to last all day. Cooking on the trail was for slowpokes; there wasn't time for eating till night came.

The early morning wind whipped against the log buildings. At that gray hour it had a lonesome sound. Lee and the old man were eating when Spargo came in from the last watch. Missy sat down to her own breakfast after giving Spargo his.

"Eat your fill, young fella," the old man advised Lee. "Then put all you can on top of that. Man's got to eat like an animal in the mountains. Pity humans can't store up food like bears. Bears'll eat till they're larded with fat. That'd make life a lot easier in the mountains when the tempertoor gets down there. Only thing wrong with it: a man'd get so fat he couldn't hardly move."

"Eat your breakfast, Grampa," Missy said.

The old man, who hadn't been eating, now shoveled in the greasy food as fast as he could swallow. He had no teeth to chew anything, so he cut everything into small pieces and swallowed without chewing. His faded eyes were bright with the thought of going into the mountains. His thin body quivered with a taut wire.

Spargo stomped his feet on the floor, making the dishes rattle.

"Cold can't be that bad, Young John," the old man said. "What you got to worry about? You'll be dozing by the stove whilst we're out there in the mountains freezin' our hind-ends off."

Spargo forked more ham onto his plate. "You wouldn't stay behind if you could."

The old man didn't like the way the ham was disappearing and he speared three pieces for himself. The platter was just about cleared, but Lee didn't want any more. Missy just picked at her food, something that didn't escape Spargo's attention. But he said nothing.

"You never said a truer word, Young John," the old man said. "Up there in the high country it's like I'm a young man again. There ain't no place like it in the whole God damned world. You can have your feather beds and potbelly stoves and all the rest of it and good luck to you. It's me for the mountains an' the free life."

Spargo grunted.

Lee was sure the old man wouldn't have asked the question if he hadn't been so excited. It came out before he knew it. "That other fella ain't comin' with us?"

Spargo gave the old man a hard stare. "No, he ain't. Changed his mind, is goin' back where he come from."

Lee didn't miss the way Spargo lowered his voice after he glanced at the bunk room door. The man had been snoring in a whiskey sleep when Lee came out to breakfast. So long stranger, he thought. Soon you'll be sleeping sounder that you are now. He guessed Spargo would kill the man in his sleep.

Spargo's cold stare had silenced the old man and killed his appetite. But that didn't last more than a few minutes and he was back to gabbing about the high country while he gummed the last of the biscuits.

"Best you be off," Spargo said abruptly, still staring at the old man. He's wondering how much longer he can trust him, Lee thought. Spargo was a cold-hearted son of a bitch and it would be a pleasure as well as a public service to kill him. That was just a thought. Spargo wasn't important. He was just a go-between, a man who leeched off others and made money doing it, but by himself he was nothing much. If the Jacks were killed or scattered, he would find something else to do. But whatever it was, it was sure to be dirty and cruel.

The last thing he said to Lee was, "Sure you wouldn't rather pay your board bill with that shotgun? I'll give you back your money and a little extra."

"No thanks," Lee said.

Spargo looked at him from behind his tangle of coarse black beard. "Mister, I could take it if I liked. This is my place and you're beholden to me. You don't know how beholden. I could take it any time I took a notion to. What do you think of that?"

The old man and Missy were mounted up. It wasn't light yet and the wind was brutal. The pack mule brayed in complaint, pulling on the lead that Missy held.

"I think you couldn't," Lee said, then wheeled his horse to follow the old man who was starting on his own. Missy and the mule brought up the rear. Spargo shouted something, but it was lost in the wind.

They followed the red-brown cliff for most of a mile and the old man turned in his saddle and pointed to a break in the rock. It didn't look like more than a wide fissure, but when Lee got closer he saw that it went clear through the rock. At first it was near dark in there, but then it began to widen and the light got better and they began to climb. It was a hard climb until they got to the top. They had come up through the inside of the cliff using a sort of natural stairway. Lee had never seen anything like it before. The cliff fell away by stages from the top and instead of going up they went down through scrub oak and blackthorn bush and the trail showed some signs of recent use. My horses have been through here, Lee thought, but it was no wonder they hadn't been able to take the whole herd. It could be done, of course, if they took the time to do it, but these were men always mindful that to be trapped too far from their stronghold was to be destroyed.

Now they were on a long narrow plateau seamed and riven by ravines and gullies. It stretched for miles and far away, past the end of it, the mountains rose up, and past those mountains were higher mountains. They were climbing step by step, though there were long stretches where the trail made a sharp descent. But inevitably it climbed again and kept climbing and after five hours travel the mountains Lee saw from the top of the cliff appeared to be no closer. He knew that was because he had never been here before; nothing up here was familiar; there were no points of reference. On the other hand, the old man—knowing these mountains—could judge distance within a few miles, that is, if he needed to judge it at all.

They rode in silence except for the old man's singing. It looked like he knew only one song and he sang the first two lines over and over: *My father was a grizzly bear/My mother was a beaver*. The first two lines were all he remembered or else he didn't like the rest of the song.

Canada geese flew over, high up, and the old man yelled and waved at them. Then he went back to singing, but now the first two lines were: *My mother was a mourning dove/My father was a gander*. His papery old voice was lost in the vast spaces of mountain and sky.

Lee wondered what part, if any, the old man and Missy had in the killing of the men Spargo rejected for Jack membership. It was hard to think of Missy as a killer, but the old man was half-savage in spite of his dead wife's book-reading, and killing would come easy to him. Whatever it was, they were there when the killings took place, and not much else mattered.

In the late afternoon, when the sky was rolling with dark clouds, Missy's horse stepped in a hole and she lost her hold on the mule. The mule ran kicking and braying through the brush, ripping the pack and scattering supplies and bedding over a wide area. This happened a few miles from the end of the plateau.

"Oh you devil, you God damned wicked devil!" the old man howled. I'm a-goin' to kill you, shoot you, hang you, cut out your black heart and eat it. Of all the miserable, cantankerous, ornery dumb-bastard craytures God put on this earth!"

The mule brayed from five hundred yards away, defying the old man, not wanting to be lost or abandoned, but showing his independence.

"Stay back," the old man warned. "I'll go argue with the rotten, evil son of satan. I think this time he's a-goin' to get it. I think at last his hour has come."

They watched from a distance while the old man edged in cautiously to where the mule was kicking up dirt and gravel. This was a scene that had been played many times before, and so the mule bolted and stopped, bolted and stopped, and the old man kept coming, holding the wide loop of the rope down by his side. He hid it from the mule though the mule knew it was there. The mule watched the old man out of the corner of his eye and didn't try for another short run until the rope swung out and dropped around its neck and was jerked tight. Then it ran the length of the rope and stopped.

"Ain't he a beauty though," the old man said when he came back leading the mule. The mule brayed, showing long, yellow teeth. "If there's a more treacherous, unreliable crayture in the Utah Territory I'd like to see it. You know why I'll never see such a beast! 'Cause it don't exist, nor never has." He continued his love song to the mule while Lee and Missy dismounted and started to gather up what they could find of the scattered supplies.

Night was closing in fast. Thunder clouds were rolling down from the north and the old man said they should leave what they couldn't find handily. Now that damage had been inflicted, the mule stood still while the old man roped and balanced the pack. They got going again.

Now Missy rode beside Lee, something she hadn't done earlier, with the villainous mule training behind. Missy had got over her shyness, or whatever it was that was eating on her, and she talked a blue streak.

"We lost the flour," she said. "But it's no use telling grandfather to get a mule that's not so wicked. I think he'd get rid of me before he'd get rid of the mule. He's a little tetched as you must have noticed by now. Sometimes he thinks that wicked mule is the same wicked mule he had fifty years ago. Claims it died and come back to earth and because it died once and came back it can't die again. He says he's going to do the same thing when he dies."

"They'll make an interesting pair," Lee said.

She gave him a stingy smile, like a miser

compelled to part with a nickel. "I guess you blame me for losing the flour. What I mean is, if you like pancakes now you can't have them. It follows that you can't have pancakes without flour."

Lee wondered if the entire Landry family might not be tetched, but if so, she wore it better than the old man. For one thing she was prettier.

"The hell with the flour," he said. "Only thing I wouldn't like as if he lost the coffee."

"The mule didn't lose the flour, I lost the flour. If I hadn't lost my hold it wouldn't have happened. You can't blame the mule. Grandpa wouldn't like you blamin' the mule. A mule is just a mule and can't help being what he is."

The storm hadn't broken yet and maybe it would pass over and break further to the west. But it was dark and cold and the wind had a real bite to it.

"He can't hear me," Lee said, "and neither can the mule." He liked mules because they were such brazen bastards. They were smarter than any horse that ever lived. Just the same, a conversation about mules had its limits. "Can we get off mules for a while?"

She was as bad-tempered as the mule. "We don't have to talk at all if that's what you want." Her face was flushed and it wasn't from the snap of the evening wind. "Would you like that? You won't talk, I won't talk. You can talk but I won't answer."

But a few minutes later she said, "Why does a man like you want to join the Jacks? If the law is after you, why don't you go to Canada or South America? Or Australia? Go to San Francisco and get on a ship."

"Using what for money?"

She had an answer for everything. "You could work as a sailor. Or you could go to the South Seas and become a slave trader. There is a great demand for slave labor in the plantations of the South Sea Islands. *The Century Encyclopedia* says many men are in that business."

Lee said, "I don't know what I'm much in favor of slavery."

"Then what about diving for pearls? You wouldn't have to dive for them yourself. You hire the natives and they dive for them. They bring them up and give them to you. A handful of pearls or just one big pearl and your fortune is made. Exporting copra, dried coconut meat, is something else you could try."

"Wouldn't work," Lee said. "I got absolutely no head for business. I couldn't give away ten dollar bills on a street corner."

"You're just saying that so you won't have to try," Missy said, and he thought it was strange, or maybe not so strange, to be getting the same sort of bullshit from her that he used to get from Maggie. Women weren't too different after all.

"Right now I'm trying to keep from getting hung," he said, wondering where in hell they were going to make camp for the night.

Without being asked, the old man answered the question. He turned in his saddle and said, "We'll be there in a minute."

The minute stretched out to more than an hour, but the night camp was worth waiting for: a deep, sandy-floored ravine out of the wind, with plenty

107

of deadwood for the fire and a run of water not far away.

Missy got a fire going while Lee and the old man watered the animals and when they got back she was laying strips of thick sliced bacon in the skillet and had the coffee cooking. It was good not to have to bend against the mountain wind and to be warm, with food on the fire.

The old man ate in his blankets, as he usually did, and he did most of the talking, but now he was tired and just wanted to sleep. "Guess I'll saw some wood," he told them. "No need to stand any watches here, young fella, not yet anyhow. In a day or two we may have some nighttime visitors, but I'll know them they'll know me. That's the trick of it, to have a lot of people know you. Ever'body knows me. That was mighty respeckful of you, calling me *Mister* Landry. You're safe as houses long as you're with me. Otherwise . . ." .

Lee built up the fire while Missy scrubbed the dishes with a hot, wet rag covered with clean sand. Then he checked the animals, especially the rascally mule which was double-hobbled and tethered to a stout bush. Missy was already in her blankets, her slicker on top, when he got back. The old man lay on his back, snoring and grunting. Missy lay with her face in shadow and didn't answer when Lee said goodnight. He lay awake for a while listening to the crackle of the fire. It hadn't rained yet, but the sky was black with clouds.

He didn't know how long he'd slept when he felt her crawling in with him. Whatever time it was, it wasn't a time for talking. Talking, even a word,

might ruin it. Missy smelled of horses and wood-
smoke and strong yellow soap. Her body stiffened
when he kissed her, but when she knew he wasn't
going to be rough with her, she kissed him back with
a fierce longing that had finally broken loose and
demanded satisfaction. They lay facing each other
in the smoke-smelling, half-light of the fire. Her eyes
were closed and she arched her back when he
unbuttoned her Levis and pulled them down over
her small, boyish backside. He slid his hand inside
her drawers and took them off. His hand moved
down to her bush and stayed there, stroking it, until
a gentle pressure opened her legs. His fingers felt
her wetness as they parted her love lips. One of her
hands was around his neck, the other groping
awkwardly until he took it and helped her to
unbutton his pants, and when all the buttons were
undone, his cock stood up like a rod. He lifted his
backside and she pulled down his pants and underpants, and moist with sweat, her hand closed over
the head of his cock and played with it. Then her
moist hand began to slide up and down his cock,
making him shudder. It excited her as much as it
excited him. So much love juice flowed from her that
the inside of her thighs were wet and she sucked on
his fingers when he put them in her mouth. She
tasted her own wild longing and liked it and her legs
opened wide as he positioned himself between them
and her hand closed on his, guiding him into her,
steadying his throbbing cock for the first thrust. He
worked the head of his cock in slowly, wanting to be
gentle, but she drove him in all the way with a
sudden bumping motion that must have hurt her.

Her muscles contracted, gripping his cock and holding it deep inside her, and then finally she relaxed and he began a steady pumping. Her legs closed around his waist and his hands kneaded her ass and he sucked her breasts while her fingernails raked his back, and if his thrusting hurt her, it was pain she couldn't get enough of.

His swollen cock would have been too big for her if she hadn't been so wet. He knew she was close to coming when she took his face in her hands and raised it from her breasts. She looked at him in wonder, this stranger who was giving her such unbearable pleasure. Her eyes were wide and staring and frantic. Now his long fast thrusts were pushing her closer and closer to the edge, and in a moment she would be over it and falling, and then suddenly she came with a great, shuddering gasp, a convulsion that seemed to spread to her toes, and her heels drummed in the sand underneath the blankets and, still gasping, she began to relax . . .

A few moments later, still silent, she took her clothes and crawled into her blankets, and he smiled at the way she wriggled and pulled until she finally got them on and then turned on her side so he couldn't see her face.

Nothing much happened the next day, and even the mule behaved himself. Thunder rumbled and the peaks were lost in clouds. All they could do was bend their heads against the wind and keep going.

The next night they made camp in a cave the old man claimed was haunted by the ghost of a mountain man who had crawled in there with a broken back after a fall from a high place. Ghost or no ghost, the old man said, it was where they were going to spend the night because the long-threatening storm was likely to break before morning.

It was a long deep cave and a draft that went somewhere took away the smoke of their fire. "As good as a reg'lar house and you don't have to do no repirs," the old man said as if he had created it himself. "Wouldn't mind livin' here the year round. Make a few sticks of furniture and call it home sweet home. More than enough space for man and animal. No snakes up this high but even if there was a few snakes they don't hardly ever bite you when they used to havin' you around. Would have to fetch water from below though there's a nice drip of water when it rains, which is most of the time so close to the peaks . . ."

Missy hadn't been to Lee's blankets for two nights and had little to say when he spoke to her. He couldn't figure her and he didn't try. Now she was kneeling by the fire putting the evening meal together. The horses and the mule were in the back of the cave eating oats spilled into a natural trough in the smooth stone floor.

The old man insisted in talking about the ghost. As usual he ate in his blankets, old and dirty and garrulous. "This poor ghost I want to tell you about," he said to Lee. "Well sir, I was the one found him right after he died. Poor man had propped himself up by the mouth of the cave, right over there behind you, I guess in the hope that some fellow human would hear his howling and might come to help him. Such a howling he put up, must have been howling for days, Lord knows, maybe weeks. Sound

111

come to me on the wind and so I figures it's only the wind squeezin' through a crack in the rocks. Then I decides that there is a real genu'ween ghost, a poor soul in torment up there. Curios'ty druv me to climb up here and take a look. Found him right there by the lip of the cave, nothin' left of him but a raggedly sack of bones. Starved to death, all the time howling for help, all the time thinkin' how he'd do himself to death and not havin' the means . . ."

Lee knew Missy must have heard this yarn at least fifty times, but now it seemed to bother her. It bothered her so much that she kicked over the coffee pot and then kicked it again.

The old man stopped talking and looked at her gape-mouthed. "What the hell did you do that for, you crazy girl? Been thinkin' on that coffee since it started to cook."

Missy kicked it again and it clanked against the rock wall. The horses whinnied, frightened by the racket. Missy yelled, "Why're you always jabbering about death and dying. Ain't you close enough to your own death to be afraid of it? You're not the last of the mountain men, you're the last of the undertakers!"

The old man winked at Lee. "Little girl, I ain't afraid of the hereafter. Ghosts don't bother me neither. Ghosts is just folks can't settle down on the other side. They're just restless and keep tryin' to come back. Some quit and make the best of it. The real restless kind keep at it till Judgment Day."

Missy had picked up the coffee pot and was examining it for holes. She had her temper under control, but she said, "Now we're going to hear all about Judgment Day."

The old man was having a good time, so good that he rolled in his blankets, making gobbling sounds. Finally he laughed himself out and sat up. Thunder rolled overhead and suddenly there was a salvo like an artillery barrage followed by a tremendous lightning flash.

"God's wrath loosed on the world," the old man shouted.

"Damn you, grandpa," Missy shouted back. "Damn you to everlasting hell!"

"I leave that to a higher judge not you, girl," the old man replied in the few moments of silence that followed the first tremendous report. He was about to say something else but the heavenly cannonade resumed.

Lee thought: He's a malicious old man, with his ghost stories and all the rest of it. He knows he is bothering Missy, yet he goes on with it.

Lee lay sprawled beside the fire with a cigar in his mouth. Taking no notice of the storm, the old man had gone to sleep. Missy was filling the coffee pot from a canteen. Home sweet home, Lee thought, but it was better than being out there in the storm. It was raining now and water ran down through the flue that carried off the smoke. A pool of water formed, but not close to the fire. Missy went on with her cooking and the instant the food was ready, the old man woke up.

The storm wore itself out after a couple of hours. The wind grew colder, the trail narrow and difficult, and there were long stretches where they had to dismount and lead the animals. They saw mule deer in small numbers and once a black bear showed itself before disappearing into a scatter of brush-choked rocks.

Lee spotted the first of the lookouts after they got across a whitewater creek swollen with storm water and melting snow from higher up. Even with fording ropes it took most of an hour before they got the animals to the other side. The lookout was high up at the top of a pile of great rocks, and though it wasn't raining and there was even some watery sun, he was covered by a tent-like oil-soaked cotton slicker of dark color that blended in with the gray rocks. Lee knew he wouldn't have seen him if he hadn't used binoculars that flashed in the weak afternoon sun. He knew, too, that the lookout was taking no trouble to evade detection.

They passed below him and the old man waved and got a wave in return. "That fella up there has a rifle with a telescope mounted on it," the old man told Lee. "And he's got one of them heliographs the army uses to flash messages from one point to another. Works in relays and works fast when there's sun. Not as fast as the telegraph line but fast enough. Was we a hostile force that managed to get this far, word would be flashing ahead of us by now. You got to give the Jacks credit for knowin' how to pertect themself."

Far ahead Lee saw what he expected to see: a vast expanse of badlands the area of which he could only guess at. It seemed to run clear to the base of one of the great peaks. Up here the eyes played tricks, but as near as he could figure it at least fifty miles of badlands had to be crossed, and that was the first really formidable obstacle any invading force would have to face. It had to be in there, in some twisted canyon, that the first war party of ranchers and farmers had met their end. It looked like a maze and was a maze of jagged stone. Up here there were no rivers that could be followed; plenty of watercourses, but no rivers. It could be treacherous even for men that knew it; for those that did not, it would be disaster.

They spent that night beside the ruin of a log and stone cabin some energetic trapper had built fifty years before. Or so the old man said.

"Fella that built it must've found damn little to trap by that time," the old man said. "The fur animals was goin' fast by the Forties. But he stayed anyhow and I guess he lived on what he could shoot. A mystery why he built it. Most trappers moved all the time, had to move as the fur animals moved, and I often think he was no kind of real trapper but some kind of a hermit with no interest in anything but bein' by his lonesome. One story is he went off to enlist in the Messican War, but I ask you how could he even know about the war, and if he did hear, how long can a war go on? I would say he just lived till he died and the animals carried off his bones."

That night after the old man had gone to sleep Missy was hacking at her hair with a steel comb. Lee watched her from the other side of the fire. Suddenly she said, "You'll be seeing the last of me in a few days. That ought to please you."

"Why should it?" Lee asked.

115

"Because I know the real reason you want to join the Jack Mormons. That's right. Deny it if you can."

"You haven't said what you think it is." If her hand even moved toward her gun he would kill her and kill the old man with the second shot. But all she did was keep hacking at her matted hair.

"You're just joining because of all those women they have. All this talk about having the law after you is horseshit. You're not running from a rope, you're running to all those asses and tits. God damn you to hell, I know what you're thinking of when you get a certain look in your eyes. You're wondering where am I going to start first? I know what you told Spargo, but you don't fool me. You can't convince me that you have to join the Jacks to escape the law. You're too smart not to be able to figure a way."

"Do tell." This was a new approach even for her, but it was better than what he had been afraid of a few minutes before. He didn't want to kill her unless he absolutely had to. He'd kill her if he had to, but he would do it with some regret. There had been good nights together and, besides, he liked her in spite of her craziness.

"You're not even a real outlaw," she said. For the moment she was cold and sarcastic and he knew that wouldn't last because she had a terrible temper. That was all right even if it meant dodging coffee pots or rocks or burning brands from the fire. All that he could handle. Just as long as she didn't reach for her gun.

"Don't you think I've seen enough outlaws and

law-dodgers to know a desperate man from a fake? You may have committed crimes, but that's not your reason for being here. Believe me, you won't get hung or shot, you'll fuck yourself to death. Like the drunkard who can't keep away from the bottle, you can't stay away from the crotch. You're nothing but a crotch fiend."

Lee didn't want to argue with her and he didn't want to get hit with the coffee pot. So he said, "I'm sorry you think that."

Her temper was rising. "Oh no you don't," she jeered. "You think you're God's gift to women. Get ready, ladies, here comes Ben Trask, the great lover from parts unknown. Spread them wide, ladies, so poor old Ben can creep into you and hide from the hangman. Shed a tear for him, ladies. If you don't like one story, he'll tell you another."

The old man made a choking sound, but she didn't even look at him.

"You sure have a mad on," Lee said.

She picked a shred of bark from the comb. "Why should I be mad? Why should I care about a crotch fiend? You don't have to listen if you don't want to?"

"What should I do?" Lee asked. "Take a stroll in the dark?"

"Yes, why don't you do that and why don't you stroll off the edge of a cliff." With a sudden angry gesture she shoved the comb into the top of her boot and jumped to her feet. Her eyes were fierce in the firelight. "You do as you please, crotch fiend. I'm going to sleep. Try anything dirty and I'll cut your balls off. You wouldn't be much good to the ladies

117

without your balls."

But for all that she came to him later. Much later, less than two hours before daybreak. She crawled in and shushed his mouth though he hadn't said anything and wasn't about to unless she spoke first. Crazy as a hoot owl, he decided. Crazy as a squirrel.

Her love-making was more like a catfight than anything else. Her nails drew blood and she slammed her crotch into his with the fury of a mad-woman. It was all he could do to control her before he thrust and let go. What now? he wondered. What will she do next?

They lay together while the cold night wind whistled through the ruined cabin and a ground-nesting bird scratched nearby. The mule and the horses stirred, knowing that morning wasn't far off.

"You don't have to go in there," she whispered when he decided she wasn't going to say anything. "You'll be a prisoner and they'll never let you go. We can turn back now before it's too late. So far only one guard saw us, the one up in the rocks. We can go back and you can sneak up on him. He watches the trail coming from the west. He won't be expecting it. We'll go all the way back, get past Spargo and get away. You saw it's a good mile from the Springs to the break in the cliff. We don't have to go past the post to get away."

Lee said, "Spargo took all the money I had. We'd be leaving without a cent. You have money with you?"

"Then we'll kill Spargo and take his money. We'll kill him from ambush and kill Lem too. There's nobody else there. God damn you, don't you hear

118

what I'm saying? Turn back or it'll be the finish of you." She took a deep breath. "It'll be the finish of me. Don't you see the sense of what I'm saying? Spargo doesn't trust banks and has his money cached in the supplies building. Gold and paper, thousands of dollars. Enough to get us anywhere we wanted to go. You can change your name and we can live for years on Spargo's money. There wouldn't be any need to rob or steal. You could start a business, make money, we could be rich. How would the law ever catch up with you? Ben Trask wouldn't exist. They'd stop looking for you. You're not that important. Will you say something for Christ's sake?"

"What do we do with your grandfather?"

"Tie him up, leave him food and water. He's a tough old man."

"How can he survive if he's tied? He'll die."

Lee could feel her anger. "Somebody will find him."

"We're way off the trail. The only travelers on it are the Jacks. He'll be buzzard bait long before they find him. A hell of a way to die."

She was silent for a good five minutes, but her anger and impatience was evident. She was out of control and knew it and didn't like it. She wanted what she wanted and here he was putting arguments in her way. She had given herself completely to a man and was furious that he didn't see things her way.

"Damn your arguments," she said. "We'll kill him in his sleep. He's old and crazy and better off dead. He can't last much longer. He nearly died last winter, so what's the difference? After he's dead we don't even have to think about him. We'll go back and deal with Spargo and go far away from Utah."

She's as murderous as Spargo, Lee thought, and as crazy as the old man. Years of loneliness and bottled-up feelings had driven her mad. No matter what she said or what she did, there would be no changing her.

"I won't do it," Lee said. "I won't murder an old man or stand by while it's done. There may come a time I wish I had, but not now. I won't do it. I'll forget we even talked about it. I wish you'd do the same."

"Son of a bitch! I won't forget it," she hissed at him. "What happened with us didn't mean a thing, did it? You just wanted to fuck me like you want to fuck every woman you can get your dirty hands on. You mealymouth bastard, I hope you get the pox from one of your women. It would serve you right."

Missy was sitting on a rock when the old man woke up and sleeved the sleep crust from his eyes. He was accustomed to waking up to hot coffee and a blazing fire. Now he blinked because there was neither.

"What's a-goin' on?" he complained. "Why ain't you fixed the fire?"

"You fix it," Missy yelled. "You and this gutless bastard can fix it. Fix your own fucking breakfast while you're at it."

Lee built up the fire and cooked breakfast and the old man, with no tact at all, allowed as how he was a hell of a better cook than his granddaughter. Missy refused to eat anything, or even to have a cup of coffee. Instead, she stuffed the pockets of her sheep-skin with jerked meat that she chewed steadily throughout the day. The old man, with no idea of what was going on, continued to make up and to sing his two-line songs. Confidentially he told Lee that Missy was just in one of her moods. She had her moods, he said, but she always got over them. He knew that because he had been dealing with them for years.

"Wasn't right, her folks not coming back to look after her. Me and the wife done the best we could, specially the wife, but a young'un needs a mother's care."

They crossed sixty-five miles of badlands in three days, and Lee tried to forget about Missy as he tried to remember this turn or that back-track of this featureless wasteland. The old man went forward without hesitation, talking to himself, singing his songs. Lee couldn't write anything down, but he didn't know that it would have helped much. The great peak up ahead was the only landmark he recognized.

No matter how hard he tried to disregard Missy, she was always there, silent, and watchful and implacably hostile. There was one night when he thought he heard her coming close in the dark and whether to make love or to kill him he had no way of knowing. But it was just some small night creature moving stealthily.

They reached the Jack Mormon settlement on the afternoon of the third day.

SEVEN

It lay in a small valley south of the peak and far from being a jumble of log houses and shanties it had a planned, orderly look and the street was plank rather than mud and on the south slope of the mountain, shielded from the wind, there were cultivated fields with people working in them in the afternoon sun. East of the town, higher up, was an earthen dam that dammed a small lake. Below the dam were gold workings or workings of some other kind, and there were people here too, all visible from far away because the air was so clear and the sun didn't have the glare of the lowlands.

"There she is," the old man said as they rode in without challenge. He waved to a rifleman in a guard tower at the entrance to the village. In the Mormon fashion, an arched gate had been built at the entrance-way that led to the main street and it was surmounted by a great wooden eagle painted gold. The eagle's claws gripped the word

PALMYRA, which had been carved from wood and was painted gold like the rest of the gate.

"Ain't that somethin' now," the old man said. "They took the trouble to do all that work right here in the back of beyond."

Lee was leading the mule because Missy had refused to do any work for the last three days of the journey. She chewed the dried meat and drank water instead of coffee, saying nothing, and at night she took her blankets as far from them as she could. Lee didn't know how things were going to go with her, but he knew she could be a real danger to him. But what he could do about it he didn't know.

The old man said they would spend the night in Palmyra and start back for Eutaw Springs the next morning. That might take care of Missy, but Lee wasn't so sure. Back at Spargo's place she had seemed wild and dangerous and ill-tempered, but now there was something else that hadn't been there before. It was too bad about Missy, Lee thought, but he hadn't shaped her unhappy life and he couldn't be responsible for it. Odd thing was that he still liked her in spite of her craziness, her willingness to murder her own grandfather, the man who had done his best to care for her for all his own madness. But he had come too far to let her get in his way and he would do anything he had to to see that she didn't.

"That there's the meeting house they're building," the old man said, pointing to a half-finished stone and wood structure that stood on the lower slope of the mountain. It was bigger than anything in the settlement. "Only they call it a temple.

123

I'll tell you one thing, young fella, these people mean to stay. Well come on now, it's time for you to meet the head man if he has time to talk to you. He may or he may not, depends whether he's at his headquarters or out somewhere lookin' over the various properties.''

Lee looked to see what Missy was doing and saw that she had dismounted. The old man said nothing and it seemed that she had the run of the settlement, was under no kind of restraint. Lee wondered where she went, what she did in a place like this. The town itself had a curious stillness about it and there was none of the aimless bustle you generally found in a small place. In an ordinary village there would be the idlers, loungers, old people sitting on porches, or just gossiping. Nothing like that here; what there was, was a kind of blankness, a dull silence, though there were men in the streets and horses in a small corral beside a blacksmith shop down the street. Then he realized why Palmyra was different from other places he'd been. Everybody seemed to have some kind of purpose, a job he had set to do. He'd seen it before in the few religious communities he'd been in, and this wasn't something he liked or admired. Here in this strange settlement, founded on hate, it was something to be feared.

The building they were heading for was at the end of the main street, a two-storey log structure with another golden eagle on top. Nothing was as finished as it would have been in a regular settlement where all the right tools were available, but it was a fair copy. Once, in a tiny village in the wild country of northern Argentina, he had seen a build-

124

ing like this. The village was dominated by a bandit who called himself mayor and the building he ruled from was a kind of miniature palace made of dried mud-brick and painted with whitewash. It looked imposing until you got up close and then you saw the cracks in the walls, the balconies that weren't balconies, the doors that weren't doors. This building was a little like that; no matter how hard it had been worked on, it was still just a two-storey log house.

They got down and hitched the animals and went in. On the second floor a young man with greased hair sat at a desk in front of double doors with hammered-iron doorhandles. Once again Lee got the impression of rough copy. This Jack leader was doing his damnedest to give the impression of the real thing. It wasn't badly done, but the fact that he bothered to do it at all told you something about the man.

The man behind the desk wore a gray coat, a white shirt, a black tie. He was less than thirty but took himself seriously. "Wait," he said when the old man told him they wanted to talk to Biship Rankin.

"Bishop?" Lee said to the old man.

"That's what he calls himself," the old man said.

"Bishop Rankin will see you," the man said when he came out. He looked at Lee without interest and went back behind his desk. The affairs of state, Lee thought. He wondered if the man behind the desk carried a gun. He had the bright eyes of the religious fanatic. Lee wondered how many wives he had.

"Bishop" Rankin sat behind his desk, a squat, hammered-down man with wide shoulders and a great shock of red hair worn long and brushed back from a protruding forehead. He looked like a big man who had been shortened by about a foot. Behind him on the plank wall was a map of Utah; looming over the map was yet another golden eagle, its talons extended. There were two windows overlooking the street and a man standing at one of them turned when they came in. He was of medium height, ferret-faced, with quick, black eyes and had the look of a man always amused at something known only to himself. He wore a black sponge suit, a white shirt, a black bowtie with the ends folded under the shirt collar. He carried a .38 Officer's Model Colt in a black belt without cartridge loops.

"Hello, Bishop," the old man said when Rankin looked up. "Brought another man from the Springs. This is him. I'll leave you now."

The old man left and Lee waited to be questioned. Instead he got a short, fiery speech from the "bishop" who delivered it sitting down. The other man stayed by the window and watched.

"I am Joseph Smith Rankin," the bishop began. "I am the temporal and spiritual leader of this community. My word is law in all matters whether they be worldly or spiritual. Transgress against community law, which is my law, and you will be put to death. There is no other punishment here. We have no fines, no jail, no second chances. Break the law and you will be excuted. Do you accept that?"

'Yes sir," Lee answered.

"Not 'sir,' " the man by the window said. "It's 'bishop.' Say 'Bishop' or 'Bishop Rankin.' "

"What is your name?" Rankin asked Lee.

Lee told him Ben Trask. There were no other questions and Rankin, obviously a madman, explained why. The old Ben Trask no longer existed, his past life had been erased as if with a pencil eraser. It had been rubbed out, the crumbs or rubber dusted away, and now the page was clean and ready to be used again. It was what was written on it from now on that mattered. What was written from that point became indelible and could not be erased.

"Which means that you will be held accountable for your actions,." Rankin shouted, suddenly excited. "You have been wilful or you would not be here. You have broken the law and escaped punishment. Here there is no escape. It is possible to run but where can you run to? Back into the badlands? Farther into the mountains? However, if you obey orders absolutely there are many rewards: absolute protection from your enemies in the outside world since your enemies become our enemies. Money, the love of good women, good food, comfortable accomodations, freedom from such vices as alcohol and gambling."

Rankin paused. "We have established here a community based on the teachings of the Blessed Joseph Smith whose name I bear, the founder of the first and the only true Mormon church. In recent years his teachings have been disregarded, ignored and even mocked at. But now—*here*—there is a return to fundamental ways. We have returned to the teachings of the Book of Mormon, which is the rock the original church was built on and so it would have remained throughout the ages if traitors and apostates had not become greedy and disloyal. We

127

could have held this land"—here Rankin waved his arm—"all this land if certain leaders had been more resolute, it they had not become faint of heart in the face of adversity, if they had not been so eager to seek accomodation with our enemies in the outside world. We should have fought the Americans when they sought to subdue us, to force us to renounce the teachings of the prophet Joseph Smith. We should have fought and died by the thousands if necessary, and if we had, we would have prevailed because God was on our side if only our leaders had the courage to acknowledge it, and God is still on our side. I tell you he is on our side here as we attempt to reestablish the old faith and the old ways . . ."

Rankin stopped talking and poured a glass of water from an enamel jug on his desk. "We have declared war on the world," he continued, "and there is nothing the world can do to stop us. Here we are invulnerable. You have seen something of our community. It is called Palmyra after the birthplace of Joseph Smith, and it is just a beginning. What you have seen has been established within a year of its beginning. We are building an army of which you will be part. We have weapons and supplies and the gold and money we have taken from the outside world. We have gold here, our own gold. For years men have searched for gold in these mountains without finding more than modest amounts. Think of it: we chose this valley not with any thought of gold but because of its location, protected from the northern storms and winds by the great mountain, and yet here we found gold. You must take that as a sign as we have taken it as a sign that God is on our side and march with us into battle against our enemies . . ."

Another pause, another drink of water, and Rankin went on with: "When these new laws were passed against us by the Gentile courts, it was argued that we should retreat to the Mexican wilderness as many others have done in the past and where they remain to this day under the protection of President Diaz. But it came to me, as the Lord came to Joseph Smith in his humble home in Palmyra, that to skulk off to Mexico would be against the word of God, a slap in the face of God. No, I cried, let us remain in our native land but find a place where our enemies cannot find us, a place where all his might is of no avail. Well we have found it here. Like the Mormons of old we have journeyed off the maps. Even now we have been offered amnesty, through intermediaries, if we will lay down our arms. I say no. Let them send as many soldiers as they choose. We know these mountains and they do not. We will fight from behind every rock and tree. Their supply lines will be thin, their line of march extended, and always we will fall back if we have to, drawing them forward into the wilderness, beckoning them to their destruction . . ."

The man at the window said, "Excuse the interruption, Bishop, but you were to inspect the new gold workings this afternoon. They're ready to release water from the dam."

Rankin looked at his huge gold watch, which lay on the desk in front of him. "Captain Wingate will talk to you," he said to Lee, and went out. As soon as the door closed Wingate sat down in Rankin's chair.

"You can sit down too," he told Lee. "Get that chair over there."

Lee took one of the chairs that were placed along the wall and put it in front of the desk. Wingate gave him a sardonic smile that wasn't very different from his normal expression. "I used to be an infantry officer," he said. "That's all you have to know about me. Now you, what did you do to bring you here?"

"Killed two men while I was stealing horses in West Texas," Lee said. "One of them was the owner's son. The father had political connections and has been using them to try to find me. There was just no good place to hide."

He repeated the story as he had told it to Spargo. "That's what happened," he said when he finished.

Wingate lay back in the bishop's big chair. The high back had been carved by somebody who knew how to work well with wood. "Well it may be what happened and it may not," he said. "It doesn't matter a damn as long as we get some things straight. Rankin may be the leader of this outfit but I'm the man who runs it. Don't tell the bishop I said that because I'll call you a liar."

Lee nodded. "You're the boss," he said.

"The bishop has his ways," Wingate said, very sure of himself, very comfortable in the head man's chair. "My ways are to make money and see that the men that work under me don't make trouble for me or for themselves. Which comes to the same thing, naturally. Now a lot of them come in here because

130

Spargo really doesn't know what I want. He knows I don't want habitual drunkards or homicidal lunatics and he's been pretty good on that score. But as to sending me men with intelligence, ruthless but intelligent men, he hasn't measured up. Not that I'm blaming him: he doesn't have much to work with, and he doesn't have time, and he isn't so very intelligent himself. Cunning, certainly, intelligent no. You can talk if you like."

Lee said, "Are there as many rules as the bishop said."

"He likes to think so," Wingate answered. "But that's because he doesn't pay too much attention to detail. Oh he can surprise you from time to time, but most of the time he thinks of the glory to come. The bishop is more than a little cracked as all men of destiny are." Wingate smiled. "But he did start this settlement and the Jack Mormons will follow him anywhere. Therefore he holds the place together because the Mormons are the strongest element here. You'll be mistaken if you think otherwise. If he gave the order they would wipe us out."

"Us?"

"Men like you," Wingate said. "Outlaws, wanted men, non-Mormons. We could take them by surprise —maybe—but that isn't the idea. Some of them don't like us, which is understandable, but it hasn't been a problem except when some horse's ass does something to cause trouble. Only yesterday I had to hang a man who raped a Mormon's woman. Can you imagine that? The son of a bitch had three women of his own, all young and good-looking enough, and he had to go and unbutton his pants in the wrong house."

"Was he drunk?" Lee asked.

"Of course he was drunk," Wingate said. "He brought it back from a raid and hid it. The hell with him! I was saying. I don't know what your plans are, but I don't intend to stay here until I grow a long white beard. But it suits me for the moment. The law is as much after me as it's after you, more so I would say, and having a certain amount of money isn't enough. I need time and a great deal of money. So you will help me and I will help you. Am I making sense?"

"A great deal of sense," Lee said. "You want men so loyal you'll want to throw money their way. Am I making sense? Do I call you 'Captain' or what?"

Wingate smiled. "I could do without the rank, but that's what they call me here. Rankin started it because I really was a captain, and everybody else picked it up. As to the question of money, yes I will want to throw money your way if you are loyal. The more loyalty, the more money. Naturally you will get your own share of what we take on the outside. Your share will be fairly small in the beginning, but I'll make up for that. Not all the money we steal finds its way into the community treasury. But don't try to cheat by yourself even if you get the chance. It's risky and I don't like it. Let me cheat for you. It's safer. I have been with Rankin almost from the beginning, so I'm trusted. If there's one thing I've learned from the politicians it's that every successful thief should earn a position of trust. You look as if you have an important question."

Lee nodded. "I do, Captain. Why are you telling me all this?"

"Simple. I need a second in command."

"What's wrong with the one you have?" Lee asked.

Wingate said, "I had to hang him yesterday. He was a good man before he fell in love." Wingate laughed bitterly, shaking his head in wonderment at the folly of mankind. "Can you believe such a thing? In a settlement teeming with women he had to go and fall in love with the wrong one. For God's sake, if he wanted a fourth or even a fifth wife he could have had her. If he didn't like the wives he had he could have changed them. But no, he wanted this woman. He absolutely had to have her and he did. He had her once. Any more questions?"

Lee said, "Don't you have other candidates for the job?"

Wingate said, "I did have until you walked in. You had a certain look about you and still do. I suppose I would have to call it confidence. You looked confident and intelligent. What you were doing stealing horses I can't imagine but"—again the sardonic smile—"we all do foolish things. I used to regret some of my foolish behavior, but it's too late for that. I don't know you and I'm sure I can trust you, but you will die screaming if you try to cross me. I mean that sincerely."

Wingate's voice was so quiet, his manner so mild, that Lee had no doubt that he meant every word he said exactly as he said it. He had no idea what Wingate had done to turn a career officer into a renegade boss of outlaws, but it must have been worse than any ordinary killing. He could not have explained why he knew that, but he knew he was right.

Wingate leaned forward in the big chair and his manner became confidential. "I intend to amass a great deal of money and to go far from the United States. What are your plans?"

"Much the same except that I might hire a smart lawyer and try to stay in the country."

"Then our goals are much the same," Wingate said. "The important thing is to be determined and steady in our efforts. Too many men come in here and become restless when they have as little as a thousand dollars. They come here because they are hunted and desperate and are glad to find a safe haven. But all too often it doesn't last, that awful feeling of being hunted, and some of them try to make a run for it while we are off on some raid. So far none of them has been successful. It would be bad for discipline if they were allowed to run off. Worse still, it would be bad for the military integrity of Palmyra."

"I won't try to run off, Captain. I know how well off I am just being here. What happens next? Do I have to be cleared for the job? Won't the bishop ask why this stranger?"

"He may or may not ask. If he does ask I'll explain my reason for choosing you. Don't let me down, Trask. It will be very bad for you if you do. I am sorry to make all these threats and I'm sure a time will come when we will laugh about them. Because of the poor fool I had to hang yesterday I

134

can't show you any special favoritism, but I will make it up to you. Like all new men you will be on probation for several weeks, but that won't last. Tonight you will have a cabin to yourself, but tomorrow you will have to bunk in with the other new men. Not a word to anyone about this discussion. Let me announce your new position as my second in command. While you are with the new men, gather all the information you can and report to me when I send for you. Any information you can pass along will only strengthen your own position."

"You suspect somebody, Captain?" What in hell was this Wingate up to? Lee wondered. Wingate had as much, or more, reason to suspect him as anybody else. But maybe that was it. Maybe this fucked up ex-officer was testing him as Spargo had tested him except that Wingate was better at it, and had more time. Wingate had said it himself: Spargo just didn't have the time.

"Let's just say that I'm careful," Wingate explained. "I want you to trust my judgment. Keep your ears and eyes open at all times. If you see or hear anything that doesn't seem right, make a mental note of it. Anything at all. Don't be embarrassed to bring it up. I'll decide if it's important. I think that covers everything."

"Captain, there are a few things you haven't explained. Can I just walk around while I'm on probation? Where do I eat?"

Wingate looked mildly surprised. "Sorry. You will have the freedom of the settlement. Why not? There's nothing to hide. Bunkhouse, call it what you like. The cabin you will stay in tonight is behind the

135

blacksmith's. A bunk will be free in the barracks sometime tomorrow. One of the men on probation is to get his own cabin and his first wife. If you get hungry, go to the barracks and the cook will feed you. Good luck, Trask. You better find your cabin before it gets dark."

It was far from dark, but Wingate held out his hand and Lee shook it. There was something strange going on, but he did as he was told and went out and down to the street. There was no sign of the old man, nor of Missy, and he wondered where they were. He was on his way to the blacksmith shop when a line of young women roped together crossed the street followed by a guard. This was no hard case guard, but a middle-aged Mormon with black clothes and a beard. The women wore shapeless dresses of some rough material and they were barefoot but didn't appear to have been beaten though the man behind them carried a short whip with a flat snake. The whip was intended to intimidate rather than to punish. The rope that linked the women together circled their waists and it wasn't pulled tight. The feet of the women were caked with dried mud and it looked like they had been working in the fields. Lee stood back to let them pass and some of them gave him defiant stares. He saw that Maggie was not among them.

"Back there," the blacksmith said in a surly voice when Lee asked him about the cabin. Obviously he was a Mormon who didn't like Gentiles even if they were, on the face of it, on the same side. Lee found the cabin and went in. There was a bed, a stove, a table and two chairs. Cut wood for the stove was stacked against the wall and there was a shelf with canned goods and a patent can-opener on it. Pots and pans and dishes were on another shelf. Everything was clean and neat and bare as a poorhouse chapel.

It wasn't cold yet so he didn't start the fire. He stretched out on the bed and thought about his situation. Wingate had tried to make their talk very man-to-man, but something was wrong there. It didn't make sense to offer the second in command job to a total stranger just in from the badlands. Just as it made no sense to have him bunk in here for one night and then join the new hard cases in the bunkhouse in the morning. He knew Wingate considered himself a very clever man, a man who knew how to play on the feelings and hopes of other men, but did he think everyone else was so dumb? Likely enough he did, and it was easy enough to understand that, given the brain power of most law-dodgers, who were generally a pretty lame-brained bunch. If they weren't so thick between the ears they wouldn't be law-dodgers in the first place and they wouldn't be found out in the second. There were some outlaws with brains, but for the most part they were small men with big ideas and no real idea of how to get out of the rut they were in. As Buckskin Frank used to say: "Most of them are two-bit gamblers trying to get into a high stakes game."

He got sick of lying on the bed and went down the street to see what the so-called barracks was like. The blacksmith, as surly as before, told him where he could find it. The blacksmith's log house was to one side of the smithy and four women, all in their early twenties, looked out the door when he stopped to talk to the blacksmith. That man must be tired after a good night's rest, Lee thought, giving the women no more than a quick glance. But the smith didn't like even that much familiarity with his wives. He yelled at the women to close the door, then brought his hammer down on the bare anvil with a mighty clang.

Lee saw no one watching him, yet he had the feeling of being watched. It grew stronger as he walked down the street. After so many years in dangerous places he had learned to respect his feelings even when there was no hard evidence to back them up. But he didn't try to find out who the watcher was because it didn't make any difference. It could even be that all the Gentiles here were under observation all the time. Wingate didn't like the Mormons, but he probably trusted them more than his own men. A Mormon was just a Mormon, while a Gentile could be anybody. Spargo did his best to ferret out spies and government agents, but he couldn't see inside a man's head. Wingate took up where Spargo left off.

Every log house in Palmyra was on either side of the main street except for one house, bigger than the others, that faced down it. That would be Rankin's, the bloody bishop watching over his flock of vultures. Apparently Rankin had been some sort of church elder before he quit or was kicked out. It was sure to have been a little of both. Men like Rankin usually brought about their own downfall, and when it finally happened, they saw it as some sort of noble sacrifice on their part. In everyday life this wouldn't matter very much, but Rankin had gone on to find his own little murderous empire. He had gone on to wage war against the world that had no use for him and, Lee decided, for that he deserved to die.

Lee found the so-called barracks, a long log house with smoke coming from two stone chimneys. It was getting dark now and light showed from half a dozen unglazed windows. There was a corral without horses behind it. Steps went in from the side and when Lee went in men sitting at two long tables stopped talking and looked at him. Then the scattered talk continued, but it was listless and there was none of the rough humor of the ranch bunkhouse or the army messhall. These law-dodgers had bitten off more than they could chew and there wasn't a poker game or a friendly saloon in sight. Lee made a quick count and came up with fifteen men at two rough tables. There were no familiar faces anywhere. A cook, a law-dodger himself by the look of him, carried in a huge two-handled stewpot and set it down.

"Come and git it," he called out.

Lee got one of the tin bowls that had been set out and took his place in line. He wondered if the badmen who had been in prison felt as if they were back there. There was very little talking on the line. Two badmen got into a mouth fight about shoving, but it stopped when the cook banged his ladle on the rim of the stewpot and warned them to shut the hell up.

Lee took his bowl of stew back to the table and sat down. The man across the table had a livid scar from the corner of his right eye to the end of his chin. He dipped bread in the stew and ate it, making a lot of noise. Up and down the table there was some conversation. One man was telling another about all the money he made in shooting contests back in Tennessee.

"You couldn't shoot your mother," the other man growled.

"I just got in," Lee told the man with the scar who had been staring at him. "How long you been here?"

"That's my business," the man said. "Why don't you mind yours? Who are you, one of Wingate's spies?"

Lee ate his beef stew and it wasn't bad. At least there was plenty of it. Then he left and went back to the cabin. Once again he knew he was being followed. But he didn't look behind him because it didn't matter.

He felt his way to the hanging lantern and lit it. Then he took off his boots and stretched out on the bed. In a while he heard horses going down the street, their hooves hollow on the plank paving. Palmyra was a progressive little community, plank paving and all. He wondered what they did on Saturday night?

Hours passed and nothing happened. It was ten-fifty-five by his watch when he decided to take off his pants and get under the blankets. He was doing that when there was a soft knock, a single knock, and the woman with red hair came in.

EIGHT

There was something familiar about her, but he had no idea what it was. She didn't look like a field worker or any kind of worker and she carried a tray covered by a napkin and in the pocket of her unbuttoned sheepskin coat was a bottle of whiskey and when she moved glasses clinked in the other pocket. She bumped the door shut with her heel and smiled at him before she set the tray down on the table.

"I'll bet they forget to feed you, you poor man," she said. "There now"—uncovering the tray—"that should make you feel better. Steak and onions and mashed potatoes. It's not fancy but it's filling."

"I had a little stew at the barracks," Lee said. "But I'm still hungry. Thanks for thinking of me."

He didn't know who she was and he didn't ask. It had to be one of Wingate's tricks, but he wasn't going to play along with it by asking questions.

"It's the least I could do," she said. "Eat up now before it gets cold."

"Well you can't be hungry now," she said after Lee cleared his plate and put a woodie to a cigar. "My name is Clarissa. They tell me yours is Ben."

"That's right."

"You must be tired after the long journey from Eutaw Springs. Some day there will be a road from there to here."

This place was full of surprises. "You think so . . . Clarissa? It's going to take some fancy engineering before that happens. As well as other things."

"Oh you mean the legal situation. By the way, would you have a cigar for me?" Lee gave it to her and lit it for her and when she puffed on it it wasn't for show. "Thank you, Ben. Everything changes and there will come a time when we are recognized for what we are, the true and original Mormons. In time the federal government will be forced to recognize the validity of our claim."

Lee looked at her. What in hell was going on? "I'm afraid all this raiding and killing won't help. I've just come from Colorado and they're even talking about it down there."

"It will change," she said complacently, disregarding what he had said. "But I'm sure you don't want to talk Mormon politics. If you're tired I won't mind if you lie down on the bed. Why don't you do that? Don't be bashful. After all, Palmyra isn't just another village. Would you like a drink?"

"If I don't get shot for taking it," he said, and she laughed. It was a nice laugh, low and musical, and, he thought, completely insincere. He had pulled up his pants when she came in and now he lay down, leaving them unbuttoned. If she wanted to look at a

142

man with his pants half-off, then she was welcome to the sight. She herself was easy to look at, this red-headed Clarissa. Tall for a woman, she was good-looking in a confident, almost arrogant way, and her full red lips were set off by her bright red hair, which was made up into a bun that didn't look in the least prissy, and her body, clothed from neck to toe in shapeless gray cotton, was as sensual as if she had been wearing nothing at all.

She filled two small glasses and took them over to the bed. "Nobody gets shot for drinking whiskey, not even in Palmyra. It's discouraged but nobody gets shot for enjoying it, not even if you get drunk. I'm very proud to be a Mormon, but our laws aren't set in concrete. Drink up now and get into bed."

Lee drank up and got into bed after Clarissa pulled off his pants and undershorts and played with his cock. "One of the things I like most about being a Mormon woman," she told him, "is the freedom between men and women. You are not a Mormon so you probably have many wrong ideas about us."

"I don't know," Lee said. "We don't have many Mormons in my part of Colorado." He was enjoying the effect of the whiskey and the feel of her hand on his cock.

"At least the Mormons aren't puritans," she said. "Mormon men and women can't wait to go to bed at night. The outside world prefers to believe that Mormon women are slaves to their husbands' lust. But what about their own lust? Plural marriage was a heaven-sent institution, a system devised by the Almighty Himself to see that no woman spent a

143

lonely life in unholy longing. There is no adultery among the Mormons who practice plural marriage, did you know that? Why should there be? If a man is not crazy he is happy with the wives he has if he comes to love yet another woman he doesn't sneak after her like a randy dog but takes her into his home as his wife, be she his third or fourth or fifth or sixth or sixteenth."

Clarissa took off her clothes as she talked and there was no false modesty in the way she took off her bloomers and tossed them over the back of a chair. Lee's cock was already rod-stiff and throbbing with the urge to get inside her.

Before she got into bed with him, she refilled the glasses and handed one to him. "Here's to honesty between men and women," she said, and knocked back her whiskey.

They made love then and it was pure pleasure to fuck a woman big and strong enough to give as good as she got. There was no need to teach her anything; she knew all there was to know about making love and yet there was nothing mechanical or false about the way she responded to his powerful thrusting. Whatever it was that had brought her to his bed didn't matter any more, or at least it didn't matter for the moment.

She was quiet in her lovemaking. She expressed her deep-felt pleasure in the way she smiled at him and sometimes even laughed happily when he did something special or unusual to her or she to him. She found humor in lovemaking and there was no shame in the things she did to him with her hands or with her mouth and later after they came several times and got into new positions she continued to enjoy it as much as he did.

At last she lay back on the pillow, smiling at him. "You have exhausted me," she said. "I am happily exhausted. Are there many more like you in Colorado? If so, it must be a wonderful state."

"There's just me," Lee said, and grinned at her.

"You have made me so happy I don't know how to thank you," she said.

"You've thanked me ten times over. A hundred," Lee said.

She propped herself up on her elbow and looked at him. "Aren't you going to ask me who I am or the real reason I came here tonight?"

"Why don't you tell me?"

"I'm Clarissa Rankin and I came to warn you about Captain Wingate."

"Oh sure, the same red hair. I thought you looked familiar. If you came to warn me about Wingate, why didn't you?"

"By the time I got here I was no longer sure I should. I thought, how can I be sure he won't tell Wingate? Now I'm sure you won't. You won't, will you?"

"Not a chance," Lee said. He would tell Wingate as soon as he saw him. She might be Rankin's daughter, but he knew this was all Wingate's idea. She had to have a real hate for her father to throw in with a son of a bitch like Wingate.

"Warn me about what?" he asked.

"I believe he intends to kill my father and blame it on someone else. When I heard of the long talk he had with you this afternoon I realized it was going to be you."

"Why me? I saw a whole bunch of new men at the barracks."

"They're just stupid outlaws without an ounce of brains between them. The other Mormons here would never believe that any of them had the intelligence or was ambitious enough to kill my father."

"How do you know all this?"

"The man Wingate hanged yesterday told me his suspicions. The rape charge was just an excuse to kill him. But there was no rape. He came here a Gentile, but converted to our faith. He loved that woman, so why would he rape her? He could have added her to his wives. An exchange of wives is common among fundamentalist Mormons who believe in plural marriage."

Lee pretended to think. "But what can Wingate hope to gain?"

"Control of Palmyra."

"But how can he if he isn't a Mormon?"

"He is a Mormon," she said. "He had to convert or my father would never have trusted him. The other Mormons would never have accepted him. Don't you see, if he can get rid of my father and hang you for it, the way is clear to taking over Palmyra. None of the other Mormons is qualified to be leader. So it would have to be Wingate."

Lee did some more fake thinking. "Have you told your father?"

"Of course," she answered. "But he is afraid of Wingate and his Gentile gunmen. He hasn't told the Mormons because there would be so much bloodshed. You may think my father is a wicked man, but

146

the villain here is Captain Wingate. It's Wingate who began the bloody raids, the burning and the killing. He is power mad and money mad. And lately he has turned my father to his way of thinking. Now that the world sees him as a bloody-handed renegade he thinks he has nothing to lose."

"Get me a drink, will you, please," Lee said. "My head is spinning with all this. This afternoon I didn't know a single soul in Palmyra. Then suddenly I'm in the middle of a plot to murder your father. God Almighty! I'm just a simple horse thief from Colorado. What do you want me to do?"

She came back to bed with two drinks. "Kill Wingate," she said, handing him the whiskey. "Kill him before he kills you. If you don't you will hang as surely as the sun will rise tomorrow."

Lee knocked back the whiskey. "Why can't you tell the Mormons and have them do it? There must be more Mormons than gunmen."

Clarissa Rankin downed her own drink. "There are but my father doesn't want an out-and-out fight between the Mormons and Wingate's men. It would tear Palmyra apart. What he wants to do is keep the gunmen under control and perhaps get rid of them altogether. Will you do it?"

"I'll think about it," Lee said. "You have to give me time to think. How can I kill Wingate without getting killed myself? If his gunmen are loyal they'll lynch anybody that tries to stop them."

Clarissa Rankin got out of bed and started to get dressed. "It's very late and I must get home before Wingate learns I'm here. Will you do it, Ben? You can do it by stealth so no one will ever know. Kill him quietly, a rope or a knife. Then take the body away at night and throw it into a crevasse. It will save your life and my father will be grateful. I'm sure he will give you Wingate's job."

"Let me think about how it can be done," Lee said.

"That's all I ask," she said, putting on her sheepskin coat. "I'll be back tomorrow night and you can tell me what you decide."

Lee made himself look worried. "Tomorrow night I'll be in the barracks. That's what Wingate said. What should I do?"

She said, "Wait for me to find you. Goodnight, Ben, and God bless you."

She opened the door and a gun spat yellow flame in the darkness. The bullet ripped through the door and buried itself in the wall. Before the shooter fired again Lee sprang from the bed and knocked her to one side. Then he slammed the door and dived after her. Now the gun fired fast, ripping the door with lead. Then—Sweet Jesus Christ—he heard Missy yelling out there in the dark:

"Ben Trask, you crotch-loving son of a bitch! Come out Ben Trask or send your whore out so I can kill her! Ben Trask, you bastard, can you hear me!"

It went on and on like that. She had fired six times and he knew she was reloading. Then the shooting began again and so did the yelling and cursing. The door sagged on its hinges and bullet-struck tin plates clattered to the floor. Lying beside Rankin's daughter he counted the shots as they came. The sixth shot struck the wall and he jumped to his feet and went crashing through the door. Just then a

148

revolver fired twice and Missy screamed and then Lee saw Wingate bending over her with a gun in hand. At the same time the old man came limping as fast as he could from the street. He had the old Henry in one hand and when he saw Missy's body sprawled in the light from the doorway he tried to raise the rifle. Wingate shot him twice and he was dead before he hit the ground.

Staring at Lee, Wingate took a handful of bullets from the pocket of his black coat and began to reload. "It looks as if she suddenly went mad," he said to Lee. His voice was quiet and unemotional. He might have been talking about a sick horse he had to destroy. "She was crazy and so was her grandfather, but I never thought I'd have to kill them. She was shouting your name?"

Lee looked at Missy's small body sprawled in death. "She was crazy to get some man," he said. "I just came along at the wrong time."

Wingate holstered his Officer's Model Colt and said, "I'll get some men to take away the bodies. Are you all right?"

"I'm all right," Lee said. "But wait a minute. I have to tell you something. Bishop Rankin's daughter came to see me tonight. She's still in the cabin and I know you sent her to test me. Come out . . . Clarissa."

She came out smiling and Wingate was smiling too. "You're a faithful lover, Ben, after all we've meant to each other. Better watch this man, Fletcher. He may prove too clever even for you."

Fletcher Wingate smiled at her and told her to go home before her father arrived. She said goodnight

149

to both of them and left. By now Mormons, but no hard cases, were crowding around the bodies. Wingate explained what had happened and told them to take the bodies away.

Lee turned to go back into the cabin and Wingate followed him. Lee poured a drink and drank it. Wingate said, "Would you have told me if the crazy woman hadn't started shooting up the place?"

Lee nodded. "I would have told you even if her story had sounded more convincing. It wasn't a bad story, but it was too complicated. My guess is you gave her a straight enough story, but she kept adding to it as she went along."

Wingate smiled his sourly humorous smile. "Something like that, I guess. But you would have told me? I have to make sure."

"I would have told you no matter what she said. I couldn't take the chance and not tell you. I find the best way to work is to trust one man and keep on trusting him until he proves absolutely and beyond all doubt that he can't be trusted. If you keep jumping from one to the other you usually end up trusting nobody. Am I making sense?"

Wingate said, "You're making a lot of sense and if that crazy woman meant anything to you I'm sorry I had to kill her."

You came up behind her and could have knocked her cold, Lee thought. Instead you chose to shoot her twice in the back.

"She meant nothing to me," Lee said. "I guess you saved my life. I didn't have my gun."

He knew this wasn't true because if Missy wanted to kill him she would have killed him. She wouldn't

150

have yelled and hollered and pegged bullets without taking aim.

"I guess I did at that," Wingate said, getting up from the table. "About your gun, you'll get it back tomorrow. And forget about the barracks. You can keep this cabin until there's a better one available. You want a wife or have you had enough of women for a while?"

"I wouldn't mind a wife," Lee said. "Where do I find one?"

"We'll go and look at the women in the morning," Wingate said.

In the morning Wingate came to the door while Lee was opening some of the cans with the patent opener. "You want to go now or later, after you've eaten?"

"I can eat any time," Lee said.

"Then let's not keep the ladies waiting," Wingate said, and handed Lee his Colt. He checked the loads and holstered the Colt and it was good to feel its weight on his hip.

"I suppose you've been wondering where the men are," Wingate said as they walked up the street in the pale, early morning sun.

"Sort of. All I saw were the new men in the barracks. I have to say they're a sorry looking bunch."

"That's the truth. I lied to you about them. Most of them aren't going anywhere but away from here. They're unarmed so the Mormons don't see them as much of a threat. The men with guns I sent out of town to take more supplies to the caves and other strong points we may have to fall back to if the army ever gets ambitious. So far it hasn't but

151

political pressure may build to the point where it has to do something. It would be a costly campaign in men and money, but the commanding general northwest may be pressured into doing something."

Lee said, "I thought that decision would be up to Washington."

"You're right. But there is such a thing as initiative. General Strater doesn't have much of that. But if he's ever replaced we may be in for trouble. That's why we have fixed a line of withdrawal. Caves in the mountains east of here are stocked with ammunition, foodstuffs, winter clothing, weapons. That's where the men are, east of here. I didn't want them here for Baxter's execution. They might have run wild and tried to stop it. Or the Mormons might have run wild and attacked them. We have an uneasy situation here at the best of times. The rape and the subsequent execution could easily have caused an explosion. It's in my interest to see that such a thing doesn't happen."

"And the men in the barracks?"

"It wouldn't have mattered if the Mormons had vented their anger on them. In fact, it might have released some of the tension and ill will that's been building up. One thing is certain. The situation here can't last indefinitely. Either the army will move or there will be open conflict between our two groups."

"And I expected to find a nice safe hideout," Lee said.

Wingate found that funny. "You still may find it. I've been thinking that it might not be a bad idea to get rid of the Mormons altogether. If that sounds ruthless, it is. It's a difficult decision to make. This is an ideal place from which to raid, but the whole thing has become too political. As a rule the government shows little inclination to become involved in the suppression of outlaw gangs. Leave that to the states and territories, the men in Washington say. But this—what we have here—has become too political. I have tried to convince Bishop Rankin to stop issuing all these proclamations of his, but he refuses. So every time there is a raid these proclamations are left behind. Nailed to doors or trees, left with rocks to weight them against the wind."

Lee thought of the tree at Spade Bit and wondered if Wingate had been there.

"To be honest," Wingate continued, "I would prefer to turn this whole Jack Mormon business into highly organized banditry. Forget about plural marriage as a political cause and concentrate on taking all there is to be taken in the shortest possible time. They say the West is changing, and of course it is, but Palmyra is an almost perfect outlaw haven in a world that is increasingly being ringed by civilization. This is the kind of place outlaws dream about, so why shouldn't it be put to the greatest possible use?"

They were now close to the edge of town and Wingate said, "We'll get to where the unattached women are in a few moments. They are housed beyond the town limits, you might say. Our little settlement keeps growing. You see I take a certain pride in the place, having been here almost from the start. But hardly a day passes that I don't regret that somehow a potentially great idea is going to waste."

"You mean turning it into a completely outlaw town?"

"Exactly. All this talk about Mormon fundamentalism and the right of plural marriage is just claptrap. It's backward looking and the government won't hold still for it. But a wholly bandit community, now there's an idea that is ahead of its time. Of course, money is the key and why shouldn't we have all the money we need."

"But first you'd have to get rid of the Mormons," Lee said.

"It always comes back to that," Wingate said. "But it's an idea I can't let go of, or it can't let go of me. Utah is a sparsely populated territory, but it has great riches. Inevitably it will become a state, but even now gold is being taken from its hills, so much that the banks of several cities, large and small, are bulging with money. A bandit army, well disciplined and trained, with a secure base, could fan out across this territory taking what it wanted. Once again, it couldn't last forever but—ah—if it only lasted a year or two. Those of us who led it would become rich beyond imagining. You could hire your smart lawyer then, Trask. You could hire a whole battery of lawyers. Yes, yes, I know. But first we would have to get rid of our Jack Mormon friends."

Lee smiled. "Rankin's daughter said you were a Mormon."

Wingate laughed. "Yes, of course I am. And I would become a Muslim if it suited my purpose."

Wingate stopped talking and pointed to a long log house with barred windows and surrounded by a stockade. "That's where you will find your bride-to-be. It isn't as terrible as it looks and not all the women in there are prisoners. The women who resist discipline are prisoners and are held there and worked very hard until they see the error of their ways. The others are there simply because there are too many of them and we don't have anywhere else to house them. It's up to you which kind you want. I'll go in with you but I can't stay. I have to see the bishop about something he has in mind."

A Mormon guard let them into the stockade and they went into the main house which was divided into two sections. Wingate spoke to the young Mormon woman, not bad looking but hard-faced, who opened the door.

"Morning, Mrs. Smiler," Wingate said. "I want you to meet Ben Trask who is to be my second in command. He needs a wife. Show him the ladies and let him decide for himself. How have the difficult ladies been behaving themselves?"

"Not too bad, Captain," the woman answered. "They know better than to get too *difficult* with me."

Wingate smiled at Lee and went out. If Maggie isn't here then I'll have to look somewhere else, Lee thought. By now she could be the wife of a Mormon or a hard case. That would make it much more difficult.

The Mormon woman called Mrs. Smiler said the women were eating breakfast, but that didn't mean that he couldn't look them over. What kind of wife did he have in mind?"

"I don't know," Lee said. "I'll have to look before

155

I decide."

"That's what they're here for," Mrs. Smiler said.
"Why don't you look at the sensible women first?'
Was I a man looking for a wife, that's what I'd do."

She took Lee to the section where the "sensible"
women sat at long tables eating breakfast. Most of
the sensible women had a subdued look. A few of
them ventured timid smiles when he came in accom-
panied by Mrs. Smiler. He wondered how many were
captives, how many were here of their own free will.
He looked them over, but didn't see Maggie.

"I'd like to look at the others," he told Mrs.
Smiler, who pursed her thin lips in disapproval, but
said nothing.

The door to the other section was bolted and Mrs.
Smiler warned him that some of the women in there
were pretty wild.

"They don't want a husband and a family," she
said. "They don't know how lucky they are to have
the chance. A lot of women never get it at all. Watch
they don't throw something at you. I'll go first to
quiet them down."

Lee went in when Mrs. Smiler called him. Not all
the women there were openly hostile; some were just
silent, lost in misery but determined to resist.
Others, the ones Mrs. Smiler called wild, started
calling him names as soon as he stepped inside the
door. Nearly all the wild ones were farm women, by
the sound of them.

The least offensive thing he was called was "dirty,
stinking, shit-faced son of a bitch."

And then he saw Maggie at the same moment she
looked up from her plate and saw him. Her face

contorted and for an instant he thought she was going to cry out and give him away. If that happened there was no way it would escape Mrs. Smiler's attention because she was right beside him. But Maggie put her face in her hands and bent her head and she might have been praying or crying or both. There was no way to tell. He stood there until Maggie raised her head again and this time her face was calm and showed no emotion of any kind.

"I'll take that one," he told Mrs. Smiler. "That young lady over there. Do you know what her name is?"

"Maggie McIvors," the Mormon woman said.

The "wild" women howled when Maggie's name was called and the Mormon woman beckoned her to leave the table and come forward. They called her every dirty name they could think of and pelted her with biscuits. Mrs. Smiler yelled at them to be quiet, but that only made them worse.

"Take her out quick," Mrs. Smiler urged. "They'll tear the place to bits if you don't get her out fast. I hope you know what you're doing. My opinion is you'd have done a lot better on the other side. This one's been a troublemaker since the day they brought her to Palmyra."

"I'll take her anyway," Lee said, smiling at Maggie who did her best to smile back. "Is this all I have to do: just take her?"

Mrs. Smiler looked surprised. "What else would there be?" She pushed the bolt into place, muffling some of the noise inside. "What you do with her now is your business. Bishop Rankin will marry you if that's what you want. If you don't it makes no difference." Mrs. Smiler did her best to smile, but it wasn't easy for her. "Mrs. Trask, that's your name, isn't it? Will you do me a great favor?"

"What is it?" Lee asked. Maggie stood beside him in one of the shapeless Mormon dressed. She had no coat and she shivered in the morning chill.

"No matter what happens," Mrs. Smiler said, "don't bring her back here. If she doesn't suit you, trade her to some other man. Just don't bring her back here."

NINE

"Wingate led the raid against Spade Bit," Maggie said.

They were in Lee's cabin and he had a big fire going and he made her drink some of the whiskey Rankin's daughter had left. She wasn't used to liquor and it made her cough. But it also brought some color to her face.

"There were about twenty of them," she said, "and they came early in the morning, so they must have been riding all night. Wingate led them and he gave the order to kill old Mac and the others. They had taken them prisoner, so they didn't have to kill them. I was there when they killed them and burned the house. Then Wingate gave the order to shoot the horses and they did. I begged them to shoot me too, but Wingate just laughed and said I was cut out for better things. I think that man hates all women. On the way back here they raided another ranch north of the Bear Lake. They shot two women there because Wingate said they were too old."

"Drink the rest of the whiskey," Lee said. "Go ahead and cry if you feel like it. No, I guess you won't. You're different, Maggie. You hardly seem like the same woman."

Maggie swallowed the rest of the whiskey. "Everything changed when I saw them shooting the horses. Those beautiful horses! I shouldn't say this, but the killing of the horses affected me more than the killing of Old Mac and the others. Is that wrong, to feel like that?"

"No, it's not wrong," Lee said. "Things take us in different ways."

Maggie said, "I was so sad when they began to kill the horses. Then after it was over I wasn't sad any more. All I felt was anger. I would have killed Wingate without mercy if somebody had given me a gun. But they're all bad, all evil men. The Mormons are as bad as the outlaws. God, how I'd like to kill every one of them. They took turns raping me on the way here. One after the other, like animals. Worse than animals. By the time I got here I couldn't feel anything. But I knew they weren't going to break me. You have to believe they haven't broken my spirit."

"I know that," Lee said.

"It's very very bad here, Lee. A woman in our part of the stockade killed herself the other night. Cut her throat with a sharp piece of glass from a broken whiskey bottle. There was blood everywhere. They fed us like pigs because the Jack Mormons think women should be strong and heavy to bear children. Being fed like that is worse than being starved. But you should have seen the women in my part of the stockade. They call them the wild ones or the difficult women. God bless them, they are wild and they are difficult. Most of them are from the farms. They would fight like men if they had the guns."

Lee had been thinking of Wingate. "What was that you said?"

"I said they'd fight like men if they had the guns. Some of them even talked about it. I'm glad to be with you, but I hated to leave them. That evil Mormon woman hates them and they hate her. I hate her so much I'd like to kill her with my bare hands. I don't care what you think. I'd like to tear her God damned Jack Mormon eyes out."

"Easy," Lee said. "I feel the same way about Wingate, but take it easy. We have to figure out how we're going to escape from here. The old man and the woman who brought me here are dead. Wingate killed them. But they knew the trail in and out of here and I don't. Just the same we've got to try."

"But what about the women in the stockade? You can't just leave them here. They'll have no chance."

Lee wondered if there was any way to settle her down. "I don't know if we can do anything about it. We'll be lucky if we can save ourselves."

Suddenly her anger boiled over. "The hell with saving myself. I don't want to save myself. Those poor women are my friends. They need to be helped. You can go if you like, but I'm going to stay. I didn't go through hell to run away from my friends."

Lee felt like a man swimming across an icy river

with an anvil on his back. He had come so far to bring this woman out and now she didn't want to go. It made him angry with the whole God damned world.

"What the hell can two people do? This may be the only chance we get. Wingate has sent his outlaws into the mountains to head off trouble with the Mormons. One of them raped a Mormon's woman and was hanged for it. But the Mormons are still ready to explode. So are Wingate's outlaws."

"I don't care about any of that," Maggie said angrily. "I want to talk about how we can save the women. I'm not just talking about the women in the stockade. I'm talking about all the women who are here against their will."

"Go ahead and talk."

"No, you talk. You know more about this sort of thing than I do. I'm asking you again. What can be used against these evil men?"

"Will you let me think a minute, for Christ's sake. There might be a chance of getting away if it came to open warfare between the Mormons and Wingate's outlaws. But I don't think that's going to happen, at least not in time to do us any good. You know where they keep the guns? Is there a place where they store weapons?"

"Yes, I do know," she said. "There are guns in that building Rankin uses as a town hall. The building where his office is. There are guns in a room on the ground floor."

"How do you know?"

"The women in the stockade talk about guns all the time. One of them was given to a Mormon who didn't like her and put her back in the stockade as punishment. This man had charge of those guns. They must still be there."

"Did she say how many guns?"

"Damn it, Lee. She said a lot of guns. Guns and ammunition. There's a padlock on the door, but that can be broken, can't it?"

"The dam," Lee said suddenly. "God damn it, the God damned dam. Wait a minute, listen to me. They just finished building a dam east of town. It's high up, it dams a small lake, they built it to work the gold diggings. Must have something to do with pressure hoses. I don't know what it's for, but it's there. Did you ever hear any explosions? Dynamite? Explosions?"

She nodded. "There were some explosions when they brought me here. I heard them one afternoon and then they stopped."

"Good. They must have been blowing down rocks and dirt from the side of the mountain. It's no use asking you if that woman said anything about dynamite?"

"She just talked about guns, Lee."

"Doesn't matter. If you heard explosions, there must be dynamite. If we can get dynamite we can blow the dam and wash away the whole settlement. The dam is filled to capacity. I heard Wingate talking to Rankin about letting some of it loose. It must be capicity-full if they're letting it spill. If we can blow the dam this town will be hit by a wall of water. There won't be a thing left standing after it passes over. Christ! If we could only get at the guns and arm those farm women. I guess you know some

163

of them will be killed if we do get the guns?"

"Of course I know it." Maggie was angry again. "Don't you think they know that and do you think they care? Like hell they care! The Jacks have been working them like dogs to break their spirit. But they haven't been able. Those women you saw me with this morning, they're out in the fields right now. They'll work there until the sun goes down. A Mormon with a whip and a gun stands over them. How do you think they feel? Do you think they're afraid to die?"

"Don't get mad at me," Lee said. "I'm beginning to think this can be done. But they have to be out of the stockade with guns in their hands before the dam blows. If not, they'll all die and we'll probably die with them."

Maggie took another drink of whiskey. "I don't give a damn. I don't care if I die as long as those bastards die with me."

"Don't be in such a hurry to die," Lee said. He wanted a drink himself, but didn't have it because he didn't want Wingate smelling it on his breath. When he looked across at Maggie he saw that she was falling asleep, worn out by the tension that had finally been released by whiskey. God damn it, she was all right. She was more than all right and she had proven him wrong. The iron he thought her character lacked had come to the forefront the minute she found herself in serious trouble. And that was where it counted most: when the chips were down.

He lifted her and carried her to the bed. She murmured something, but didn't wake up. He covered her with a blanket and sat down to think. Damn it, it could be done if all the parts came together at the same time and if they had the right amount of luck. You couldn't succeed at anything if luck wasn't with you. Being in the right didn't always bring luck, but he liked to think it did.

Someone would have to lead the women while he set the charges and buried Palmyra under a million tons of water. That meant Maggie unless there was some women in the stockade who could do it better. He didn't think there was.

They would have to be safe on the high ground when the wall of water hit. That meant the mountain slope where the fields were. But they couldn't be just on high ground, they had to be far up the slope, almost as far up as Rankin's God damned temple, when the dynamite-powered flood put an end to this evil place. He felt the old hot anger coming back as he thought of Wingate and Rankin and all they had done, all the human misery they had caused. He thought of decent ranchers and farmers he hadn't known and never would know because they were dead. He thought of the two women Wingate had murdered north of Bear Lake. Because they were too old, Wingate said.

He felt there would be no justice at all if Rankin and Wingate didn't die with the others. But he forced himself to be calm. He would do the best he could; he would kill them if he could. That was the idea: to kill as many of the bastards as possible. But he couldn't risk the lives of everyone just because he wanted to kill two men who deserved to die, if anyone deserved to die, and so he would give it up if he had to. But if by some chance they happened to escape, well then he would have to catch up with them in some other place and at some other time. It was as simple as that.

He didn't know how much store he could put in his position as Wingate's second in command. Nothing was for sure. But right or wrong he would have to take it for granted that Wingate now trusted him and wanted him for the job. It could all be some elaborate lie, but he would have to assume that it was not. It was the only way he could put this plan into action.

First he would have to get into Rankin's town hall to see if the guns were there. Without the guns they didn't have much chance of pulling it off. The flood probably wouldn't kill every Mormon, every outlaw, and so there would be shooting. How much depended on how many men survived the flood. That some of the farm and ranch women could shoot he had no doubt, but how many could shoot well enough to go out against men? But they couldn't shoot at all if they didn't have guns. He would have to move fast because the Mormons, meaning the bishop, could remove the guns and ammunition at any time. With open warfare a very likely possibility Rankin might play it safe and move the weapons to a more secure place, where Wingate's men couldn't get their hands on them.

Breaking the women out of the stockade was another, different problem. According to Maggie the stockade was guarded day and night by a single guard whose position was just inside the gate. One man didn't mean much provided he could be killed silently. If he got off as much as a single shot the entire plan would be ruined. He knew he could trust Maggie to lead the women, but he didn't think she'd be able to kill a guard without making a sound. Well she might, of course, that is, if she got close enough and the guard was unsuspecting. That would free him for the work on the dam. He decided that it would be better all round if someone else killed the guard.

The dynamite presented the most difficult problem because he didn't know where it was, and there was even the possibility that all the dynamite had been used up during the blasting. No dynamite, no damn busting, no escape. Of course Maggie would insist that the women would fight anyway. Sure they would. They'd probably fight like tigers, but would it do any good, and the answer had to be that it would not. No matter how hard they fought, they would be beaten in the end.

Maggie woke up and asked what he was going.

"Planning the escape," he said, and he asked her if she thought she could kill the guard at the stockade. Then he explained how it had to be done, quickly and without noise. "I don't know if you'll have to kill that Jack Mormon woman. Is she armed?"

Maggie said, "She has a pistol, but she doesn't carry it into the dormitory. She's afraid somebody will take it away from her. Yes, I can kill the guard and I can kill her too. I want to kill her. It will be a pleasure to kill her."

"I told you to go easy," Lee warned her.

"I can't go easy, I don't want to go easy. What do you care how I am if I get the job done?"

167

"Suit yourself, Maggie. Just don't get everybody else killed. I think you have to be the one to lead the women back to the town hall to get the guns. Can you do it?"

She nodded. "I can do it."

"And later if there's fighting? What then? You've never fired a long gun in your life."

Maggie looked defiant. "Then I'll lead them with a pistol. I've seen you shoot a pistol at Spade Bit. I know how to load and fire. You point it and pull the trigger."

Lee grinned at her. "That's how you do it all right."

"What else do you want me to do?" Maggie was showing more fire than he'd ever thought possible. No matter what happened after this, she would be all right, a new woman, tough and brave and strong. The whiner and the house proud nag who wanted to be liked by "respectable" people was gone for good.

He told her about taking the women high up the mountain slope.

"You may have to fight your way up. They'll forget you're women when they see you have guns. The Mormons will show less mercy than the outlaws. The outlaws may or may not be in the settlement. Just don't expect any mercy from the Mormons. The sight of women with rifles will drive them wild. They're used to having women fetch and carry for them. That makes them think they have bigger balls than other men."

A few weeks before Maggie the prig would have objected to that kind of language. Now she just smiled.

"We'll shoot their big balls off if we get the chance."

"Move along the side of the mountain while the flood is boiling through. Head east and try to make the badlands before the flood ebbs. It's a small lake and the flood won't last all that long. I'll follow along as soon as I can. But make for the badlands. If you have to you can make some sort of stand there. Above all keep going, always heading east. Once we're in the badlands we'll all be equal. I don't know if I can find a way through any better than you can."

"Yes, but what if there is nothing to run from? If the flood destroys them, why should we lose ourselves in country where we may be lost for good?"

Lee smiled at her. "Then all you do is move east along the mountain and wait for me. Let the escape plan go for a while. There's something else I must ask you to do. You may find it harder than anything I've asked you so far."

She looked puzzled. "Such as?"

"I want you to be pleasant to Wingate when he calls. He'll be sure to come by to see what kind of wife I've picked. Can you do it? It's important to keep on his good side. The plan can't succeed unless I can move around freely. Maggie, do you hear what I'm saying?"

Instead of giving him an answer she stared into space. Her eyes narrowed and her face turned pale. She must be reliving the whole thing, he thought.

"Maggie, answer me. If you can't be pleasant to Wingate I'll try to head him off. I didn't mean you

169

have to kiss him and treat him like your dearest friend. Can you be civil? That's all I'm asking."

"All you're asking! I'm sorry, Lee. You're doing your best and I'm being dramatic." She sounded very tired. "Yes, yes, yes! The answer is yes, I can be civil to the dirty fucking cruel son of a bitch. I can be civil to him, but don't ask me to be more than that."

Lee said, "That'll do fine. He'd be suspicious if you were more than that. He may be suspicious anyway. Wingate is a suspicious man."

"If you can call him a man."

"Makes no difference what you call him. We need him for now. I know somebody was watching me the night the old man and his granddaughter were killed by Wingate. At the time I thought Wingate was behind it, but it could just as easily have been Rankin. He may be moving to protect himself. I have to find out who was following me or I won't be able to check on the guns."

Maggie was sitting by the fire with a blanket wrapped around her and he knew she was dreading the arrival of the man who was responsible for her degradation at the hands of the Spade Bit raiders. He had asked her to be "civil" to Wingate, but hadn't asked himself how he would take Wingate when he came to the door. He knew he could keep himself under control, but he would have to do much more than that. Since Wingate became his friend a sort of easy familiarity existed between them and the other man even made his little sour jokes about the Mormons and their ways, and that morning, walking to the stockade, he had done an impersonation of Rankin's speaking style that would have been funny under normal circumstances.

It was hard to think of Wingate as lonely, but he couldn't think of any other word to describe him. He seemed to have a need to talk not only about the situation in Palmyra but about himself, as if talking convinced him of his own importance, and when he talked of the huge amount of money he needed to leave the country, there was the feeling that he really didn't want to go because he would then be finally on his own, cut off from the past which he claimed was of no importance and yet seemed to haunt him.

Lee knew that Wingate's claim on his friendship might be genuine enough, yet it did not necessarily prevent Wingate from regarding him with deep suspicion. This wasn't all that hard to understand, but it could make it difficult to know when Wingate was just making a casual observation or when he was saying something with some deeper purpose behind it.

Maggie would have said that he was taking too much time trying to figure out Wingate's character when all that was needed was a bullet through his head, but he knew it was worth the effort because it was the only way he could even guess at how Wingate would behave in some future situation. So far he could only conclude that Wingate was a man who saw too many sides of the same question for his own good. The Mormons were a threat because their open defiance of the federal government would inevitably bring retribution and so the only logical thing was to destroy them, yet he always hesitated at taking that final step. Sending his force of outlaws to the mountains when he should by right have kept them in the settlement for his own protection and as proof of his power was another example of his reluctance to meet an important decision head-on, and while this kind of thinking might have been understandable in a civilian it was a puzzle when the man involved had been trained as an officer, someone accustomed to making decisions and then carrying them out . . .

Lee looked up and so did Maggie when there was the crunch of boots in gravel and a knock on the door. He nodded to her and she nodded back. She was ready to meet the man she hated more than any man in the world. Lee opened the door and Wingate stood there black-suited and sourly smiling and he said, "Well, let's have a look at the new wife, Trask. You can't have come back without picking one." He came in still smiling and when he saw Maggie his smile didn't change and didn't fade, and he said in a hearty voice that didn't suit him, "So this is the little woman."

Maggie stood up slowly and Lee said, "Maggie, this is Captain Wingate."

Maggie bent her head and Wingate said, "Please call me Fletcher. It's an unfortunate name but it belonged to my father and he decided to share some of his humiliation with me."

"I am pleased to meet you," Maggie said, and her lips were as drained of color as her face.

"The pleasure is mine," Wingate said, and Lee thought: God damn it, he doesn't even remember her or he's pretending he doesn't, but even as he looked at Wingate he knew he wasn't pretending. His smile was too casual to come from anything but indifference. He's playing the gentlemanly officer to the noncom's wife, Lee thought. He really doesn't remember her.

"I'm going to steal your husband for a while," Wingate told Maggie, still playing a part that didn't suit him. Maggie nodded stiffly and they went outside.

Lee got ready for questions about Maggie, but none came. "I just got word that the men are returning to Palmyra without orders," Wingate began.

"Maybe your information is wrong," Lee said, but Wingate cut him off with, "My information is not wrong. They are returning without orders and how soon they get here depends on how fast they travel. I'm assuming they'll get here some time tonight."

"You think they'll be trouble?"

"I don't know. It depends on how the Mormons see it. The men have had time to think about Baxter's execution. My information is they suspect me of selling them out to the Mormons. They don't realize I had to hang Baxter or the Mormon would have risen up and slaughtered them."

"What do you want to do, Captain?"

"Wait until they get here, they try to reason with them. That won't be easy, but I have to try. The worst news is they've been drinking. No, my information is not wrong. They've been drinking."

"Where would they get liquor in the mountains?"

Wingate gave Lee an impatient look. "It's not hard to make moonshine, raw alcohol. All you need

173

is copper tubing, some kind of mash, a fire. It can be made out of almost anything. You must know all that. They had plenty of time to make it between raids and now they're drinking it and threatening to kill all the Mormons. That may be just drunken talk or they may really intend to do it. The hell of it is they're our men and we'll have to back them if the Mormons start shooting at them. Some of the Mormons have wanted to get rid of us for a long time. They resent outsiders, any and all outsiders. There may be nothing for it but to seize Rankin and hold him as hostage. We'll seize their leader and seize their guns at the same time. Then we can bargain or try to. If that fails we'll hang onto Rankin and pull out of here."

"What guns are you talking about?" Lee asked, not liking the sound of this. "I would have thought each Mormon had his own weapons."

"Of course they do, but they also have a large reserve of rifles where Rankin has his office. You were there. That building. They're downstairs in a storeroom. Dozens of rifles, thousands of rounds of ammunition. The rifles are just sitting there. We have to get at them if a shooting war can't be avoided. The hell of it is they may grab it first. Damn that Baxter and his hot cock! He may have fucked us into a war."

It wasn't like Wingate to use obscenities and Lee could see how agitated he was. Seizing the guns would be an act of war that Wingate wanted to avoid.

"You know who the rabblerousers are?" Lee asked. "You know which of our men are trying to

174

force a fight with the Mormons? Every mob has its leaders?"

"Ferguson is," Wingate said. "He has his supporters, but he's been behind this all along. He's a thug and a bully and he was one of Baxter's closest friends. They belonged to the same gang in Montana. I should have done away with him when I had the chance, but he's loud and brash and well-liked by the other men. He's wild and dangerous but Baxter was able to keep him in line because they were friends. He's the one who's leading the men back here. I don't know how to stop him short of killing him. And if I do that the men will turn on me."

"I'll stop him," Lee said. "You won't have to kill him and you won't have to seize the guns unless you want to."

Wingate stared at Lee. "You don't even know Ferguson. How can you stop him? He's bigger and heavier, and stronger than you are. What do you think you're going to do, challenge him to a fist fight? He may not want to fight you with his fists or feet or anything else but a gun. He may just whip out a gun and kill you. Get into a fight with him and they may all pile on top of you. You're talking like a madman."

"I'll find a way to stop him," Lee repeated. "He can't be so much of a monster as you say he is."

Wingate was seething with impatience. "Talking to you is like talking to the wall. I'm telling you he'll kill you. Baxter told me Ferguson has killed and crippled men in saloon fights. Can you say the same? Of course you can't. The man is not civilized even by the standards of his kind."

"Let me try it," Lee urged. "Isn't it worth a try if it means buying us time? That's what you want, isn't it? You said yourself a shooting war with the Mormons can't be won. At least it can't be won the way things are now."

"No, it can't be won the way things are now. We'll wait until they get back and I'll try to reason with them. If that fails then you'll have your chance at Ferguson. Of course the Mormons may attack without warning and we'll be glad to have men like Ferguson on our side. You better lay low for now. That's what I'm going to do. You don't have to wonder what time the men will arrive. You'll hear them long before they get back."

Lee went back inside and repeated everything to Maggie, who looked alarmed when he told her he was going to take on Ferguson.

"He may kill you," she said. "Wingate must know what he's talking about. He knows this man and you don't. Don't do it, Lee. We'll find another way to escape."

"There is no other way," he said. "We need those guns, but if Wingate seizes them that's the end of it. Ferguson isn't John L. Sullivan, for Christ's sake. He's not the wild man of the woods. He's just a man."

"John L. Sullivan wouldn't try to bite off your nose," Maggie said. She didn't smile. "John L. Sullivan wouldn't try to break your spine. Give it up, Lee."

He didn't know where she got her information, but he knew she was right about Ferguson. Saloon

176

brawlers used every dirty trick they could think of: teeth, boots, broken bottles, everything and anything. Biting off ears and noses were commonplace. Eye gouging was as common as drunken salesmen in day coaches. But if you expected all that, had seen it before, it came as no surprise.

"He may seize the guns no matter how your fight with Ferguson comes out," Maggie argued. "You may get killed or crippled for nothing. Then what will happen to me?"

He smiled at her. Women always said that when all else failed. "You'll be fine," he said. "You're one of the wild women from the stockade and nothing's ever going to get you down. You said that yourself, or have you forgotten so soon?"

"I have forgotten that you used to be pretty good in bed," she said. "Why don't we get under the blankets so I can make sure you haven't lost your touch?"

Later she said, "All right, you pass the test. However, there are other tests I would like to make . . ."

TEN

Lee was pulling on his boots when he heard them coming and they sounded like Texas cowboys at the end of trail, barreling into town with three months wages in their pockets. Their howling echoed up and down the valley, but there were no gunshots. At least they had enough sense not to push the Mormons too far.

"Be careful, Lee," Maggie called from the bed.

He put on his hat and went up the street to the log barracks where he knew Wingate would be waiting. Wingate was a vicious son of a bitch, but he wasn't a coward. He'd be there, ferret-eyed and sourly smiling.

"Let me talk first," Wingate said, stepping out of the shadows.

The street was deserted and there was a moon, but clouds threw shadows on the side of the mountains. Up above the great peak hung over everything. Mormons might be watching, but they didn't show themselves. Lee eased the Bisley Colt in his oiled holster. As Wingate said, this thing might not be decided with fists.

The yelling came closer and soon they could see them coming in from the end of town, thirty-two likkered-up hard cases swaying in their saddles, drunk and angry and loaded for bear. Moonlight glinted on the liquor bottles in their hands and they traded obscenities. One man started to belt out a dirty song, but was shushed by the others. They had the solemnity of drunks, but these drunks were armed to the teeth. Lee and Wingate stepped into the street where they could be seen.

"That's Ferguson with the white Stetson," Wingate said before they got close enough to hear.

Lee saw a man about his own age, but wide and big and heavy. He was so big that he seemed to dwarf the big Morgan horse he was riding. Even on a horse and still at a distance he had the look of a man who kicks down doors and throws policemen through windows.

Ferguson was out in front and he saw Wingate and Lee before the others. He said something to the man closest to him and they all reined in. Lee and Wingate walked toward them.

"Well goodnight there, Captain," Ferguson called out in a low loud voice that didn't have much intelligence behind it. "Out for a stroll in the moonlight, are you, Captain? Who's your lady friend? Or should I say, Who's your gentleman friend? You do have gentleman friends, don't you, Captain? Anyhow, that's the rumor that's been going round. Nasty things, rumors, except with you they ain't exactly rumors, are they?"

So that was the trouble with Wingate, Lee thought. A few sneering words from a saloon brawler had explained everything.

"What are you doing back here, Ferguson?" Wingate said. "I told you to stay out there until I sent for you. You know what can happen here? They're ready to attack us, they want to attack us. Now take the men and go on back to the supply base. You have everything you need there. I see you have plenty of liquor. What's all this drinking about? I never knew you to be much of a drinking man."

Ferguson took a swig from the bottle in his hand. "Well you see, Captain, this is kind of a special occasion. Kind of an Irish wake so there has to be plenty of liquor. We're mourning the untimely death of our dear friend Tom Baxter. You heard of him, I'd say. You oughta heard of him. You hanged him, you man-loving son of a bitch."

The hardcases laughed and jeered, but Wingate stood his ground. He flipped his coat behind the butt of his Officer's Model Colt and his hand dropped to his side. "If you'd like to back up that kind of lying dirty talk with gunplay, here I stand. Come on Ferguson, make a try for your gun."

Ferguson just laughed and had another drink. "We all know how good with a gun you are, Captain, and you won't find me making the mistake of going up against you. That, sir, would be suicide. But that don't mean I'm the least bit afraid of you. You are ten times a better shot than I am and you can shoot me any old time you like only you'll be full of lead in three seconds. Isn't that right, boys?"

There was a chorus of approval and Ferguson said, "Captain, we're all through taking orders from you. As of this moment your little outlaw army is disbanded, meaning that you can go soak your head in a shit bucket. We're not going back to any God damned mountains and we're not going to check any God damned supplies. What we're going to do is stay right here in good old Palmyra and have ourselves a whale of a time. We're going to fuck all the ladies and kick the asses of all the men. And if they want to start shooting at us, well then, Captain sir, we're just going to have to shoot back. Tit for tat, like the girl said to the soldier. Now get out of our road, Captain sir, or we'll ride all over you."

Wingate turned to Lee. "Any time you like," he said.

Ferguson leaned his bulk forward and cupped a hand to an ear. "What was that you said to your gentleman friend, Captain sir? What's your name, Gentleman Friend? Are you of the same persuasion as Mr. Wingate?"

"Least all I don't fuck my mother like you, pig-face. That's right, you fuck your mother because your mother is a scabby whore that sucks cocks for a living. How'd you like them apples, pig-face."

Ferguson was so startled that he just looked down at him. This bear of a man was being grossly insulted by a man ten inches shorter and a hundred pounds lighter and he just stood there instead of running for the hills.

"What did you say?" Ferguson sounded so astonished that some of the hard cases chuckled. "Shut up!" he roared. "Everybody shut up. I see a cockroach standing in front of me asking to be stepped on."

"Try it, pig-face," Lee dared him. "Climb down and try it. I'm as good with a gun as the captain, but I'm not going to shoot you. Climb down, you tub of pig shit."

Ferguson was so heavy that it took him a while to dismount. Then he walked toward Lee, all three hundred pounds of him. "I'm going to tear your head off and cork your ass with it." He uttered other fanciful threats. "I'm going to tear your leg off and beat you over the head with it."

He was reaching for Lee when Lee drew the Bisley and cocked it right in Ferguson's face. The muzzle was only a few inches from his forehead, so he could see it. It was cocked and Lee's hand was steady. "All you have to do is grab it," Lee said. "It's cocked and this pistol has a hair trigger, but you might get lucky. Take a chance, pig-face. If you're fast enough you can grab my hand with both of yours and so stop the hammer from falling. I've seen that done, so I know it can be done. But speed is what counts. I'll give you thirty seconds to think about it."

There wasn't a sound as Lee held the pistol steady as a rock. Ferguson had been half-drunk, but he was sobering fast and though the night was cold beads of sweat ran down his booze-reddened face. One of the drunk hard cases called out, "We going to let this son of a bitch treat Fergy like that." Another man, less drunk, told him to shut up. Lee started talking again.

"What's the matter, pig-face, got no guts. You got a whole sackful of gripes but no real guts. Your pals want you to do something but you're letting them down. What's happening to Fergy the iron man? Why looka here, pig-face Ferguson done shit and pissed his pants. If you can get hold of my wrist you can snap the bones like twigs. But you got to take the chance, pig-face."

Ferguson's eyes rolled up to look at the barrel of the Bisley and his huge fists clenched and unclenched without doing anything. "Get a move on, Fergy," Lee said. "You get hold of me you can bend my spine till it snaps, you can toss me clear over the top of that mountain. All the things you were going to do to me, why ain't you doing them? I'm getting tired of this, Fergy. I'm going to pull the trigger in a minute. Goodbye, Fergy."

Lee pulled the trigger and the flat sound of the hammer fallling on an empty chamber echoed in the silent street. Ferguson didn't move and neither did Lee.

"Now the next one may or not be live," Lee said matter-of-factly, "but of course you have no way of knowing that. Now I got an offer I want to make to you. You want me to pull the trigger of do you want to strip off our clothes and do a dance buck nekkid. Don't see why you got to be shy about it seeing as how all your friends are here. I'll count to five and while I'm doing it you decide what it's going to be. One . . . two . . . three . . . four . . ."

"I'll dance," Ferguson said.

"Can't hear you," Lee told him. "Repeat after me and say it loud. I'm a big teddy bear and I want to dance for my liddle friends. Repeat after me and say it loud. I'm a big teddy bear and my iddle pecker swings when I dance. Repeat after me and say it loud. I'm a big teddy bear and sometimes I like to eat shit."

With one quick movement, Lee stepped back from Ferguson and ordered him to strip or get shot through the head. Lee taunted him with, "If you don't want to strip, why don't you tell your pals to open up on me. See, Fergy, you don't have the balls of a flea. Get off your clothes, Fergy, or do I start counting? One . . . two . . ." Ferguson began to take off his clothes. His large size pants dropped to the plank-paved street, revealing a very dirty pair of underdrawers. One item of clothes followed another until Ferguson stood naked in the middle of Palmyra's main street.

"Dance," Lee ordered. "Dance and sing, Fergy, your pals want some entertainment. Dance and sing. I'm a big teddy bear and I want to dance for my iddle friends." Ferguson began a slow shuffling dance. One or two men laughed, then the laughter spread through the gang of hard cases and there were whoops of approval or disapproval, and it was just as Lee had thought. Ferguson had enemies as well as friends.

Lee pointed the Colt at Ferguson's face and told him to dance out of town. "Just go as you are," he said. "Leave your clothes. I said leave them right there in the street. Don't come back, Fergy. If you come back I'll shoot you on sight."

Huge and naked, Ferguson stood there helplessly. "You can't do this. I'm cold. I can't go out there without my clothes. Some of you men help me."

"I'm going to kill you in ten seconds," Lee warned. "Now dance on out, Fergy. Dance and sing: 'I'm a big teddy bear and I want to dance for my friends.' Go on now, it's not so hard."

Lee waited until Ferguson disappeared into the darkness before he looked at the rest of them. He said, "You men go back to where you were and don't come back here till you're sent for. Do it now."

There was some hesitation but it disappeared as soon as he holstered his gun and turned his back to them. This was their chance to blow him to bits. But then he heard them turning their horses. Wingate was still there and he said, "You did it all right. Where did you ever learn a trick like that?"

"On the Mexican border. A local badman was terrorizing a small town and nobody was able to do anything about him. Then they hired a town tamer and instead of killing the bully he made him strip in the plaza right in the middle of the day. He probably found clothes somewhere, but he never came back. If Ferguson comes back I *will* kill him. What do you think, Captain?"

"It's over for now," Wingate said. "You've made yourself a lot of enemies tonight. But you know that."

"I know it and I don't care. It wouldn't have worked any other way. One shot and we'd be dead now. You want me for anything else?"

"Are you in such a hurry to go home?" Wingate asked.

185

"It's the time of night for it."

"They'll be thinking you're the one to obey," Wingate said.

"No, I don't want anybody to obey me. You're the captain as far as I'm concerned. Goodnight."

Lee walked away and Wingate called "Goodnight" after him. There wasn't a sound as he walked back to the cabin. He had carried off this bit of bravado, but he knew it had been a fluke. Ferguson had buckled but another badman with more pride might have defied him even with a cocked gun in his face. Ferguson had been a bully for so long that he hadn't ever really been tested. Being tested was what made a man tough.

"What happened?" Maggie said when he came in. "I kept waiting for the sounds of guns going off."

Lee told her what had happened and she turned pale. "And Wingate just stood there?" she said.

"That's what he did," Lee said. "The outlaws are gone, but they may not stay gone. It was the shock of what happened to Ferguson that made them leave town. Every man there was thinking, 'I don't want that to happen to me.' When I say thinking I don't mean really thinking. Men like that fear humiliation more than anything else. Sooner or later they'll know it couldn't have happened to them. They may decide to come back and kill me. Or when they get halfway sober they'll see the sense of not getting into a shooting match with the Mormons. You never can be sure what outlaws are going to do."

"So that's what Wingate is," Maggie said. "No wonder he hates women. I can feel it now, what's wrong with him. The trouble that brought him here must have had something to do with that."

"Probably. There must have been a killing or a number of killings. But I'm just guessing. Forget about what he did. We don't have much time. If I can find the dynamite we'll do it tomorrow night. If there is no dynamite we'll burn the town and try to use that as a cover. We'll have the Mormons after us, but if there's to be an escape it has to be as soon as possible. Tomorrow night may be too late, but I don't see how it can be done any sooner. I'm going out now to see if the guns are there."

"Wingate may be watching," Maggie said. "I know I said all those things, but I was talking about myself. I don't want you to get killed. What if Ferguson is waiting for you in the dark?"

Lee shrugged. He was tired of Wingate and the Mormons and Palmyra and everything. "If he comes back it will take him time to work up to it. You take my gun and watch yourself. If Ferguson comes in that door you shoot and keep on shooting. Aim at his chest. It's a big enough target. Just don't shoot me when I come back."

"How long will you be?"

"Not long," Lee answered. "It's just down the street. I just hope there isn't a guard. I'll have to think about what to do if there's a guard."

There were some Jack Mormon houses behind the houses that lined the main street. One good thing about Palymra: it had no dogs. He moved quickly without making a sound. No lights showed anywhere. Moving and then stopping to listen, he got to the back of the town hall in a few minutes. The building stood squat and dark and ominous. He edged toward the door and found it padlocked.

He climbed to the second floor using notches in the logs as footholds. In place of glass the windows had hinged shutters that opened out. He tried two windows and found the shutters bolted from the inside. A third shutter was looser than the others and he used his knife to slide back the wooden bolt. He left the shutters open to give him light. He was in Rankin's office, with its big desk and carved chair. He went downstairs with a ring of keys he found in a desk drawer. The door to the gunroom was sure to be padlocked.

There were rooms on the ground floor, but the only one with a padlock on it was under the stairs. There were only three keys on the ring and the second one he tried opened the lock. He pulled the lock loose and went into darkness that smelled of gun oil. The room had no windows and he struck a sulphur match after he closed the door. There they were, the guns, all rifles, no handguns. They lay in factory cases. One case had the lid pried up and he picked up a rifle, a .44 caliber, the one with the long barrel. The rifle was new and had recently been cleaned. So had the others in the case. He put the rifle back.

Cases of ammunition stood against the wall. He had to light another match, taking care to put the charred stub of the other one in his pocket. And then, moving the light, he saw the case of dynamite. The case was open and some of the sticks had been removed. It was a hell of a place to store dynamite, but he saw that the sticks were new and not at all sweated. Stick dynamite wasn't like liquid nitro. It wasn't dangerous if you didn't expose it to too much heat or rough handling. They said it was possible to hit a stick of new dynamite with a hammer without causing an explosion. Lee had never tried that.

There were primers and fuses to go with the dynamite. He put four sticks and primers and a length of fuse in the pockets of his coat and looked around to see if he had left any signs of being there. There were none.

He put the padlock back in place but didn't lock it. It looked all right if you didn't look too close. Unless somebody checked it during the day it would be the way he left it when the women came for the guns.

He went back upstairs and put the keys back in Rankin's desk. Then he went out the window and used the knife point to bolt the window. Five minutes later he was back in the cabin after calling to Maggie before he opened the door. She was in a chair with the cocked pistol in her lap. He took the pistol and let down the hammer and holstered it. Her eyes grew wide when he showed her the dynamite.

"We're getting there," he said. "We'll go tonight. Are you sure you'll be able to go through with it? If you can't do it, say so now. It'll be too late after we get started. Answer me. Can you do it?"

"Yes, I can do it."

"It has to be a knife. This knife." He showed her the long-bladed skinning knife he always carried in his boot. "Take it, get used to the feel of it."

She took the knife and turned it in her hand. The lamplight was reflected in the blade. "I'll be all right," she said. "What time will it happen?"

189

"Late," he said. "After they've gone to bed. I'll give you my watch. Get the women out of the stockade and go along behind the houses on the main street. We'll walk around today and I'll show you where the town hall is. The front door will be padlocked and you'll have to tear it loose or break down the door. Those big farm women ought to know how to break down a door. But get it done because you have to be on the mountain when the dam goes up. The rifles are new Winchesters and are easy to load and shoot. Couldn't be easier."

Her eyes were bright. "We're finally going to get away from this horrible place."

"If all goes well," he said. "Here's how it will go, allowing for setbacks. Ten o'clock should be late enough. We'll leave here together. I'll head for the dam, you for the stockade. I'll give you a full hour and a half to break the women out, take the guns and start climbing the mountain. But make sure you have the rifles loaded before you start across the street. You'll be out in the open then and there's the chance you'll be spotted. If somebody challenges you don't try to do anything but kill him. Just open fire and keep shooting. You'll have all the ammunition you need, so just keep shooting. But get up on that mountain. That's the most important part of all. There will be nothing left of the town when the water hits."

"We'll be up on the mountain if we have to crawl there."

Lee smiled, feeling better now that he had the dynamite. "Run, don't crawl. Anyway, walk fast. Like I said, move along the slope and wait for me. If

190

I don't show up after the water goes down, head for the badlands."

Maggie stared at him. "Then we head west and keep heading west."

"It's the best you can do," Lee said. "If the flood destroys the Jacks we can come back and try to find what we can. It would be hell to start back without supplies. But that part has to come later. First we have to get out."

"Yes," Maggie agreed. "First we have to get out."

In the morning, they walked along the main street and he showed her where the town hall was. The doors were open, which probably meant that Rankin was in his office. Above the town the dam stood like some kind of fortification. On the way back they met Wingate heading for the town hall. "Morning," he said to Maggie, touching the brim of his hat.

"I'm going to talk to Rankin," he said. "It may still be possible to avoid trouble. I'll point out that the men have gone back to the mountains. That should convince the bishop that we have no intention of trying to seize power."

Lee thought it was strange to hear Wingate use such expressions as "seize power" when he was talking about a miserable little settlement populated by renegade Mormons and ragtag outlaws. "I hope you can convince him," Lee said, thinking of the dynamite he had hidden back at the cabin. He hated to let it out of his hands, but it was too bulky to carry around even in the big pockets of his coat.

They went back to the cabin and waited for night to come. Maggie said, "I keep thinking of all that's

191

happened during the last few weeks. Less than that. It just seems like a long time. Remember how I used to talk about wanting to be invited to the houses of nice respectable ladies. We would have library parties and talk about the latest three-volume romances."

"I remember," Lee said, checking the primers. The door was closed and a chair back was wedged under the doorhandle. "Why not. Ladies are entitled to talk about books. But I know what you mean. Sometimes you were a pain in the ass."

She laughed. "I suppose I was. Thinking back on it I'm surprised you were able to put up with me. But I was good in bed, wasn't I?"

"The best," Lee said. "Why are you talking so much in the past tense? We'll go back to Spade Bit after this is over."

"We may," she said. "Or I may go somewhere else. I don't know that I wouldn't go back to being a pain in the ass."

The primers were all right and he put them away. "I don't think there's much chance of that. You've been through hell and it's changed you. For the better. People who change as much as you've changed hardly ever change back. Some of the old habits and ways come back, but that's only natural and doesn't matter a hell of a lot. Spade Bit is always there for you. It's your home."

"We'll see," Maggie said. "Whatever happens I know I'll be able to take care of myself. I couldn't before or I didn't try. I'll be all right."

They went back to talking about the escape because it was directly ahead and could not be avoided and so they had to talk about it. They both knew they might not live through it and these might be the last hours of their lives. Even now with death looking them in the face they knew they were an ill-matched couple and there was nothing they could do about it. But they had the escape in common and they had more than that. Looking at her he felt great affection and regard, and though these feelings were new, they were strong and would last.

"You are in charge and don't let anybody take away your authority once you get started," Lee told her. "I may not be with you when you start back west. Some woman may try to take away your authority because people are like that no matter what the situation is. There can be only one leader and that has to be you. Things will fall apart if you aren't strong."

"I'll be strong," Maggie said.

"Be strong tonight," Lee said. "After you leave the stockade don't let anybody go their own way. Some of those women are crazy and full of hate and may want to do wild things. Yes, I know I shouldn't talk like that about your wild women, but that's what they are: wild. Don't let them start burning the town or killing Mormons. They'll just get killed and you'll get killed and probably I'll get killed."

Maggie laughed in spite of the situation. "You certainly are cheerful, Mr. Morgan."

"You don't know what it's like when these things get started. There's a wildness, a madness that has a life of its own. Once the killing mood takes hold of people they don't know when to stop or even how to stop. Keep a tight rein on those women of yours."

"You make them sound as if they belong to me."

"Tonight they do and they may belong to you for a long time after tonight."

"What about Wingate?" Maggie said abruptly. "What if Wingate gets away?"

"What about it? I'll find him no matter how far he runs. Now that I know he was at Spade Bit it's a lot simpler for me. I had to know who was at Spade Bit and now I do. The other men who were there aren't so important. I can't spend my life hunting them down. Wingate will have to stand for all of them."

Maggie frowned. "I'm not like you, Lee. I can't look at things in long terms the way you do. I want justice now."

"You mean revenge," Lee said. "No real difference when you think about it. I'm not sure I want either. For me it's gone beyond that. I just want him dead or, to put it another way, no longer among the living. He shouldn't breathe the same air as other men. For me it's as simple as that. But you must put him out of your mind. There is no guarantee that we can kill him now. It's what you want and I want, but we can't dwell on it."

Maggie looked grim. "I dwell on it. I dwell on it all the time. I don't know that I'll be able to pick up the rest of my life knowing he's still alive."

"You'd better. Because I'm tellling you there may be no way to kill him. The flood may get him. Would that be enough for you? If he drowned in the flood. A lot of men are going to go under in that flood. Why should Wingate float to safety?"

Maggie said, "No, it wouldn't be enough, but it would do. It would have to do."

194

"Indian women were always worse than the men," Lee said. He smiled at his bloodthirsty woman from Massachusetts. "Forget about Wingate. Leave Wingate to me. You have to concentrate on leading your women to safety. Now there may not be enough rifles to arm all the women . . ."

ELEVEN

They waited into the evening and the sun went down and there were no sounds at all. Lee went outside and from the front of the cabin he could see the mountain and the great peak looming over it and when he went back inside Maggie had the knife in her hand and was looking at the blade.

"I'm getting used to it," she said.

He sat down and looked at his watch and it was nine-forty, so there were twenty minutes to go before they started out. He knew they could have started now, but he had said ten o'clock and they might as well stick it out. His horse was saddled and waiting outside behind the cabin. It didn't matter if Wingate came now and asked what the horse was doing there. Wingate could be killed and the body hidden.

Once again he checked the dynamite, the primers, the fuse. The fuse was already cut and everything was in place. He had cut long fuses, ten minutes fuses, that would give him time to head for the mountain where it sloped down to the dam at that point. It was too bad Wingate didn't come now so that business could be settled once and for all, and he wouldn't have to think about it any more. But Wingate didn't come and when he looked at his watch again it was five minutes to ten and he told Maggie it was time to go.

Outside, he eased the Colt in its holster and tucked his coat back behind the butt. With Maggie beside him, he led the stallion down to the street and they started toward the east end of town. He took care leading the horse, but even so its hooves made a clomping sound on the plank paving. No one was in the street and there were no sounds except those the horse made. He didn't see Wingate, but that didn't mean he wasn't there.

Facing the street, Rankin's house still showed lights and it looked like the bishop was up late. They reached the end of the street without being challenged and it was time to go their own ways. Off to one side the stockade was, a long, squat shape in the darkness. Maggie had the knife in the sleeve of her coat and she nodded when he asked her one last time if she was ready to do it.

"Go on," she said. "I'll be all right." She looked at the watch and it was ten minutes past ten. She hurried away from him and he mounted up and rode out in the direction of the dam. There was no planking here and the horse made little noise. Lee climbed down when he was a hundred yards from the dam because there wasn't time for scouting and coming in slow and careful. The dam bulked up big in the darkness and if there were guards they had themselves well hidden. But there were no guards because, there was really nothing to guard the dam against, and then he was right under the great thick wall of the dam. The wall went up from nearly seventy feet and he could hear the lake water lapping on the other side of it, at the top.

He placed the charges and waited, listening for sounds. There were none. He counted time in his head. He guessed half an hour had passed by the time he checked the charges again. He couldn't see the stockade from where he was, though it was less than a mile away. A low hill got in the way and cut off his view. But Maggie and the women had to be out of there by now, heading for the town hall and the guns.

He counted off more time and knew that most of an hour had passed. Fifteen minutes later, or what he took to be fifteen minutes later, he saw small dark figures on the side of the mountain. He took binoculars from his pocket and was able to see by moonlight. More and more figures went up the slope from the town. He waited while they climbed higher and higher and as he waited he kept counting. One last figure climbed the slope and after that no more came. That was all of them.

He had touched off the fuses when there was a wild howl from far out in the darkness. Then he heard the thunder of a lot of horses coming fast. Jesus Christ! Wingate's men were coming back except they weren't Wingate's men any longer. He looked at the fuses, all burning down fast. Out in the dark the howling grew louder and then they swept past in a black cluster of men and horses. They swept down into the town and guns started to go off. He didn't know if they were just loosing off bullets or were being fired at. It was too far to see. All to the good, he thought. They were all together now. All together in Palmyra.

He mounted up and headed for the mountains. The slope was steep where the dam was and he had to urge the stallion to make the climb. He was halfway up now, not yet safe from the flood when the dam blew, but he was getting there. From where he was now he had a good view of the town and it looked like the Mormons and the outlaws were finally at it. Guns blazed all along the main street and the hard cases might have been trapped. He couldn't see that far. The stallion was stumbling and kicking when the dam blew.

The four charges blew like small blasts of cannon-fire and the dammed-up lake literally fell forward. A great wall of water seventy feet high crashed forward and swept down as if a mountain had fallen. As he watched from high up, the town just disappeared. The enormous cliff of water didn't just flood the town, it swept it away like the hand of God. Then as the first great wave flattened out and passed over, the water covered the highest home and pushed it along in front of it. Lee started along the side of the mountain and then he was high up over the town. Except the town no longer existed. It was gone.

He rode along the mountain looking for the women, but they were well ahead of him. Now when he looked down the water was settling into a lake that would ebb and empty and dry-out as time passed. But for now it was a lake, flat and black in the moonlight. Nothing floated on it that he could see, but he was high up and the moon was down for the moment and there may have been bodies that he couldn't see. Well that part's over, he thought. He had come a long way to do this, and now it was done. The Jacks would raid no more.

He caught up with the women about a mile from what was left of the town. Lake Palmyra he thought of calling it. The women were strung out along the side of the mountain and up ahead he heard Maggie shouting for them to stay together. The women he caught up with carried Winchesters and they panicked when they turned and saw him and he had to do some shouting himself before they lowered the rifles. Maggie turned and walked back toward him and her eyes were alive with excitement. She carried a Winchester and she shook it at him like an Indian.

"We did it, Lee, we did it. We saw them fighting, heard them fighting down there and suddenly they were swept away. The water hit the town and it just disappeared. I feel as if we've won a great battle."

"Not yet we haven't," he said. "Tell the women to hold up. Now we have to go back and see what we can find in the temple."

Maggie talked to the women and came over to Lee. "They don't want to go back. They hate the place so much they don't want to go back."

"Tell them we're going the hell back. Ask them if they want to die of starvation in the badlands. That's what'll happen if they don't go back. We may have to go all the way west to the mountains to get

200

supplies. Tell them to simmer down. You simmer down too."

They went back along the side of the mountain, the women fearful and reluctant. A climb up to the half-built temple turned up nothing. It stood there in cut-log grandeur, but it was empty. They were coming down the slope when he heard shouting down below and a tough looking farm women said to Maggie, "They've caught somebody."

Maggie went down ahead of Lee and then she called back. "They've captured Wingate. Do you hear what I'm saying? They caught the half-drowned son of a bitch."

Lee rode down and saw Wingate surrounded by women with rifles. He had pulled himself out of the water and had been caught doing it. Now he stood wet and shaking with cold and his beltgun was gone and so was his head. He didn't look like a leader of men. He didn't look like any kind. His already dull eyes dulled even more when he saw Lee.

Lee dismounted and walked to the man who had burned his ranch, slaughtered his horses, killed his friends. Lee had his gun drawn, but he put it away. The women cried out when they saw him holstering the Colt. The women crowded around again, clawing at Wingate, spitting in his face. His face was bloody with scratches and one ear dripped blood where it had been torn at the lobe.

"Kill me," he said to Lee. "Don't let them have me. Draw you gun and kill me . . . please."

"Not a chance," Lee said and turned away. A rock struck Wingate in the face and he dropped to his knees begging for mercy. Another rock struck him, and another, and another. Lee looked at Maggie and she had her face turned away.

"It's not so easy when you have to look at it," he said.

"The hell with you," Maggie said and stopped to pick up a rock. She threw it as hard as she could.

"Feel better now?" Lee said, but she didn't answer. Instead she went back to the women and stopped them from mutilating the body.

They waited on the side of the mountain until the sun came up. During the night it was cold, but nobody complained. The women, cold and hungry, had an air of satisfaction that Lee could understand, but didn't feel himself. Down below the floodwater was receding and what was left of the town came into sight. There wasn't much left, log stumps standing in the mud, a pile of rocks from a toppled chimney.

"We'll have to go west to the mountains," Lee said. "We'll be going the wrong way, but there's no help for it. When we get the supplies we'll have to come all the way back. That's the way wars are fought. This was a kind of war, I guess."

"But we won it," she said.

It took them three days to reach the caves where the emergency supplies were stored. The Mormons had put them there, thinking to use them in a retreat. There was food and winter clothing, weapons and other supplies. They stayed there for a day while the women rested and the supplies were laid out for the long journey west.

"We'll just go and keep going," Lee said. "An old man and a crazy woman brought me in here and now

I have to try to remember everything about that journey."

They started back early in the morning and at that hour the women looked tired. The war was over, with another, longer war dead ahead. "Keep them moving," Lee told Maggie. "They were fine during the escape, but now they feel let down and some of them will want to give up, but you can't let them because no one will come to help them and they'll just die."

They passed through Palmyra for the last time and Lee was glad to look back and see nothing. There were bodies in the mud and buzzards were busy. They started down into the badlands and two women died there before they finally found their way out of the rocky maze and were heading due west again. The supplies held out, but they made very bad time because the women were so tired. Another woman died, but she had been sick and would have died anyway. Then, because the pace was so slow, the supplies began to give out and everyone was put on short rations. There was a light snowfall and brought some hardship because they had no tents; there were places where firewood was scarce and that had to be rationed too.

It would all have been bearable if the women hadn't started bickering among themselves. Women who would have fought bravely against a common enemy now fought among themselves. Women who liked and admired Maggie at the start of the journey now resented her and some hated her. Lee, trapped in the middle of all those women, felt himself at a loss. He longed to be back at Spade Bit in the company of men: Sid Sefton and Bud and Charlie and Wes, listening to their bragging, their horse gossip, their dirty stories.

Maggie always came to him for support, but he didn't have much advise to give about women. "You're the boss," he would say. "You handle it." And she did handle it as best she could, but the role of the pioneer leader was new to her and as time went on she liked it less and less. One night, sitting by a meager fire, she said angrily, "Damn it, Lee, I'd rather be back in Massachusetts." Then she smiled and said, "See, I'm changing back to my old ways. Don't you hate me for it?"

"Just don't start hanging curtains on the mountain," he said, and they both laughed.

The supplies ran out and Lee shot a mule deer, but that didn't go far, and the meat was gone by the next day. Game was scarce in the mountains. It was there if you had time to look for it, but there wasn't time. It was late for snow, but that didn't mean it wouldn't snow. Lee remembered what Spargo said: "The weather doesn't run like a train schedule," and he was right: it snowed the next night and most of the next day and it was hard to start fires with damp wood, and there wasn't all that much wood to begin with.

"Maybe the would have been better off back in the stockade," Maggie said one night when she was feeling low. "There was plenty to eat and Mrs Smiler didn't beat them if they behaved themselves. You said it would be hell, but I didn't listen to you."

"They're free," Lee said, "and those that make it back will be glad they're free. Some more are going to die, but that can't be helped. If you can even get half of them back it will mean something. Only thing to do is keep going and hope we'll make it."

It snowed again and this time it didn't stop for two full days. It could be worse than that, Lee knew, and probably would be. Another woman died and they piled rocks around the body and left. No one had the strength to dig a grave for her even if there had been shovels.

Hunger and cold hammered at them as they bent their heads against the wind and kept going. Maggie seemed to be everywhere, helping women who had fallen and couldn't or wouldn't get back on their feet. Lee did what he could, but it wasn't much.

He figured they were about halfway back to Eutaw Springs. But it was still too far and he wondered if any of them would make it. They had camped in a brushy gully that provided some protection from the wind driven snow, but now it was morning again and the women were refusing to go on. They sat huddled in blankets with the snow on top of them, frozen and listless and despairing.

"It's no use," Maggie said. "They won't move. Do you think there's any chance of getting help?"

"Not a chance in the world," Lee said. "The closest place is Eutaw Springs and that's where Spargo is. Besides, I'd never get back in time. I'm going out now to see if I can shoot something. In the snow, there's not much chance. You want me to be honest. That's being honest."

He had gone several miles west of camp when he saw them coming from far off. It had stopped snowing, but there was fog and visibility was limited. They were at least half a mile away, a line of men coming down a long slope. Spaces out between them were pack mules and horses. They were all afoot because the slope was broken ground and the slope was steep. Infantry, he thought. A big party of infantry.

He rode out to meet them and they disarmed him before the officer in charge, a major, listened to his story. The major, a short, grizzled man in his forties, thought he was a renegade and wasn't inclined to believe him.

Lee was patient; he could see the major's point of view. "The women will tell you," Lee said, and they did. Only then, while the women were being fed, did the major open up.

"I'll have to continue on to the Jack settlement, but I'll send a detachment of men back with the women. You say it's gone, wiped out," the major said. "Sorry to hear that. I was hoping to engage the bastards."

"Yes, Major," Lee said, glad that he didn't have to fight anybody. "It's gone. For good."

The major, whose name was Catlen, said the Territorial Government had finally been forced to move against the Jacks. "We're militia," the major said. "But there will be regulars coming."

Lee didn't say they weren't needed because the major would not have liked it. He didn't say that the Territorial Government had sat on their fat political backsides for too God damned long.

"We arrested that man Spargo," the major went on. "He will be tried and hanged. We found graves, many graves. He is on his way to jail right now. I'm sorry to hear that an ex-officer was mixed up with this dirty business. You say his name was Fletcher Wingate. Never heard of him. But it could be an alias."

They had an infantry escort for the rest of the journey and when they finally reached Eutaw Springs the trading post had been boarded up and Spargo was gone. Lee thought of the men he had killed there, all the rootless outlaws who had died there. It was good to see the last of Eutaw.

After that the rest of the journey was easy. Lee and Maggie parted company with the women at the Logan Road and then went north to Idaho and Spade Bit. The men came running when they saw Lee and Maggie and Lee said, "Later, later" to all their questions.

There was a cabin, not fancy, but new. The horses were in corral, the ruins of the house had been cleared. A new house would go up there when he had the money. He would have to work hard now and make house-building money. It was good to stand and breathe the clear mountain air, to smell the pines and know that it was all over.

Maggie stayed for three weeks and then said goodbye and went away. She said she thought she would go back to Massachusetts, but she wasn't sure. Their lovemaking had been as good as ever, but he could see the old Maggie coming back. More and more of it returned with every day she stayed. They both knew it would soon be what it had been and that was no good. Everything worked fine for them as long as there was a common danger to be faced. But now the danger had passed and they found they had really nothing in common. It was a pity, Lee thought, but there it was: it couldn't be changed. Maggie felt it too, but she said it was all right. She was the same and yet she wasn't, if he knew what she meant.

Lee said he did.